INTO AFRICA

Thomas Sterling

HORIZON • NEW WORD CITY

Published by New Word City, Inc.

For more information about New Word City, visit our Web site at
NewWordCity.com

American Heritage Publishing
Edwin S. Grosvenor, President
P.O. Box 1488
Rockville, MD 20851

1
MUNGO PARK:
EXPLORER

The great river was silver-gray and sluggish in the mid-morning heat. Its banks were low, and on the opposite shore, a large town could be seen. The buildings, square and made of mud, boasted flat roofs. Some were two stories high, and many were whitewashed. From a distance, they stood out like a mirage, receding and approaching in the glaring light. Graceful minarets soared above the narrow streets. That was how the African town of Ségou appeared one July morning in 1796. A young man named Mungo Park sat in the sand by the river, watching the huge canoes, which had been carved from logs, carrying hundreds of people and even horses across the current to the market. He was twenty-five years old, alone, without funds, and starving. But in his diary, he noted that he took "infinite pleasure" in the scene. More important, he noted which way the river was flowing: east.

The river that the young Scotsman was gazing at was the Niger, which had been a cause of wonder and speculation for centuries. The classical Greek historian and geographer Herodotus had reported, in his *Histories* in 440 BCE, a great river flowing eastward in this western part of Africa. But even Herodotus had not seen this river for himself. His description of it came from the account of an African chief, who in turn had heard about the river from some traveling tribesmen who claimed to have seen it.

More recent geographers held contrary opinions; they assumed that the river must flow west and have some connection with the Nile. These rumors were started by the geographer Leo Africanus, whose *Descrittione dell'Africa (Description of Africa)* was published in 1550 – nearly 2,000 years after Herodotus's account.

A Muslim born in the Islamic Spanish city of Granada, Africanus was the first to use the word "Niger" to describe the river. Many have mistakenly interpreted "Niger" as meaning black or negro. In fact, the name probably originated from the phrase "*ger-n-ger-*," which in the Berber language indigenous to North Africa meant "river of rivers."

Africanus supposedly had discovered the river while traveling with an uncle on a diplomatic mission into North Africa. He had reached as far as Timbuktu, a city then part of the Songhai Empire, which he described as a center of trade in gold, ivory, books, brightly colored cloth, and slaves. The "rich King of Timbuctoo," he wrote, "hath many plates and scepters of gold, some of which weigh 1,300 pounds." And nearby, according to Africanus, the great Niger River flowed from the east to the west. Mistaking the direction in which the Niger flowed would hamper future explorations, at least until Mungo Park corrected it.

The "fabled" city of Timbuktu sparked the imaginations of European adventurers, lured by the promise of gold. Many searched but never found it. A group of London businessmen formed a company in 1618 hoping to establish trade with Timbuktu. The first expedition never returned, presumably massacred by African tribesmen. Because of Africanus's description of the Niger as a westerly river, the explorers sailed up the River Gambia, believing the two streams would connect – or even that they might be one and the same. Other expeditions barely made it back, greatly diminished. Those explorers who did return were gravely ill from being forced to drink urine and even blood to survive the barren Sahara Desert. After these unfortunate adventures, "Timbuktu" became synonymous with "lost city."

This did not stop adventurous men from wanting to find it. Whether for business or geographic exploration, and in spite of the odds, they pushed for more trips to find the source of the Niger and there, they hoped, Timbuktu and its gold. Mungo Park's assignment was to find the source of the Niger and there, presumably, the lost city. His earlier exploits were what led him to this voyage.

Park may have seemed an odd choice to lead an expedition into Africa. Born in Selkirkshire, Scotland, he was the seventh of thirteen children of tenant farmers. Young Mungo was tutored at home, before attending grammar school. His parents, devout Protestant Calvinists, intended for him to enter the Church of Scotland, perhaps as a priest. But, though his faith was strong, Mungo gravitated toward science and medicine. When he was fourteen, he became apprentice to a Selkirk surgeon named Thomas Anderson, whose daughter he would later marry. At the University of Edinburgh, he studied medicine but also botany and natural history. Soon, he realized that he was more interested in plants than people. For a year after graduation, he worked in the field of botany with his brother-in-law, James Dickson, who was a gardener and seed merchant in London's Covent Garden. It was through this work that Park got his first taste of adventure.

In 1788, James Dickson, the brother-in-law,

had founded, with fellow botanists, the Linnean Society – named for Swedish naturalist Carolus Linnaeus, and dedicated to the study of natural history. One of Dickson's partners was British botanist Sir Joseph Banks, who twenty years before had been part of Captain James Cook's expedition to discover Australia. Banks became acquainted with Dickson's young assistant, Mungo Park, and was instantly impressed with his eagerness to learn. When, in 1793, the Linnaean Society sponsored an expedition to the western Indonesian island of Sumatra, Banks recruited Park to be his representative.

On the Sumatra expedition, Park's role officially was surgeon's mate. Actually, he was a plant collector. In February 1793, Park sailed aboard the East India Company ship *Worcester* to Bengkulu, on the southwest coast of Sumatra. There, in 1714, the British had built Fort Marlborough, which had never been profitable as a trading post. But it turned out to be a boon to Park's career.

Park spent nine weeks on the coast of Sumatra. When he returned to London in 1794, he gave a lecture to the Linnaean Society in which he described, among other things, eight species of Sumatran fish that he had discovered. Though his findings were not published until three years later, they were sufficient to impress Joseph Banks, who pushed for Park to lead another, greater expedition.

Banks had his sights set on the interior of Africa, which was still almost entirely uncharted – so much so that it was called the "Dark Continent." In June 1788, around the same time that the Linnaean Society was getting its start, Banks also founded the African Association. (Formally, the group was the Association for Promoting the Discovery of the Interior Parts of Africa.) Its mission was to discover the origin and course of the Niger River, and thus the way to the lost city of gold, Timbuktu. This marked the true beginning of the age of African exploration.

Banks's first choice to lead an Africa expedition was an American named John Ledyard. Born in Connecticut, Ledyard had sailed as a young seaman on trading ships to Gibraltar, the Barbary Coast, and the Caribbean. Then, jumping ship in England, he had joined the British Navy as a marine. From 1776 to 1780, he had sailed on Captain James Cook's third and final voyage, reaching Hawaii, where Cook was killed by natives. After a failed fur-trading venture, Ledyard had set out from Paris on a bold adventure – backed by Joseph Banks, as well as Thomas Jefferson (then American Ambassador to France) and the Marquis de Lafayette. He had proposed to explore the American continent by first crossing Russia overland to the Bering Strait, heading south through Alaska, and then across the American West. But he was arrested in Russia, by order of Catherine the Great, and eventually deported to Poland. By June

1788, Ledyard had made his way back to London. He was downtrodden, and completely broke. But his spirit was somewhat revived by the news that the African Association was recruiting explorers.

Ledyard had gone to his friend Joseph Banks and proposed an expedition across Africa, from the Red Sea to the Atlantic Ocean. He was a more than capable candidate, having survived years at sea and in previously undiscovered territory. So it was not a difficult decision for Banks.

Ledyard had sailed from England that June of 1788, and arrived at Alexandria, Egypt, on the Red Sea, in August. There, he formed a caravan that was to head into the interior of the continent. Before it departed, Ledyard wrote to his sixty-year-old mother, Abigail, that he expected to be gone for three years, after which he hoped to visit her in Connecticut. In his letter, he reported that he was in "full and perfect health" although he had "tromped the world under his feet, laughed at fear, and derided danger." But that was the last that Abigail Ledyard heard from her son, whom she would outlive for sixteen years. The caravan was delayed, and before it could leave Cairo, John Ledyard had become ill. In an attempt to relieve his symptoms – a "bilious complaint," as he called it, that caused hacking coughs – he inadvertently poisoned himself with a fatal dose of vitriolic (or sulfuric) acid. Thirty-eight years old when he died,

Ledyard was buried in a modestly marked grave in a sand dune where the desert meets the Nile River.

Though Ledyard's death was mourned on more than one continent, it did little to stymie the enthusiasm of the African Association. In fact, while Ledyard was still traveling, another expedition to Africa had set out.

The second expedition was led by a little-known explorer named Simon Lucas, who was about as different from Ledyard as it was possible to be. Lucas, unlike Ledyard, was not an adventurer, but a lifelong civil servant – paid an annual salary of eighty pounds as courtier of England's King George III. As a child, he had been kidnapped by Barbary pirates and kept as a slave for three years before being ransomed back to the British. During that time, he had learned Arabic, which made him valuable to the king's court as an interpreter. His language skills also had played a part in his recruitment by the African Association.

In October 1788, Lucas had landed his expedition at Tripoli, in present-day Libya, on the northwestern edge of the African continent and about 1,000 miles west of Cairo – where his colleague and competitor, John Ledyard, was deathly ill. But it was fear - not illness - that ended Lucas's expedition. He had hired guides to take him across the Libyan Desert, but after encountering tribal wars that continually delayed the journey, those guides soon abandoned him.

Lucas was afraid of being captured and once again becoming a slave. So, only a few hundred miles after setting out, he gave up the expedition, turned his camel around, and went north to the Mediterranean. He limped back to London with little to offer the African Association for their investment.

Soon after Lucas's return, another explorer tried and failed to reach the Niger River. Daniel Houghton, an Irishman, had been a foot soldier and then lieutenant in the Irish military. To support his large family after retiring from the military, he had accepted the post of engineer to the Nawab of Arcot, which ruled the Carnatic region of South India. But on the way to India, his ship crashed at the island of Gorée, off the coast of Africa. There, Houghton established a fort, where he held the post of major for four years, while learning the native languages of Arabic and Mandingo. That experience was a factor in his selection, in 1790, by the African Association to lead an expedition up the Gambia River to chart the continent's west coast.

Despite his failure to find the lost city of Timbuktu, Houghton did venture farther into the interior of Africa than any European had before. Following the Gambia, he passed through the present-day city of Barra, a trading post at Pisania, and the kingdom of Wuli, where he was received cordially by the local ruler. But then, a string of bad luck followed. A devastating fire in March 1791 destroyed the town of Medina, where he was staying, along with most of Houghton's equipment and weapons. Tribal wars broke out that delayed his expedition. When a local trader named Madegammo offered to take him to Timbuktu in exchange for much of what he had left, Houghton was in no position to refuse. They set off in July 1791. That September, Houghton sent a dispatch to the trading post at Pisania; he was never heard from again. Supposedly, after two days on the Sahara, Houghton had become paranoid that his traveling companions were trying to kill him. He turned back south alone without food and water and died of starvation.

It was two years before reports confirming Houghton's death reached London. By then, the African Association had already decided to capitalize on his discoveries by partnering with the British government to install a consul in the territory along the Gambia later dubbed Senegambia. That consul, James Willis, was to develop good relations with the local kings – in part, by gifts that included muskets. That, in theory, would help open trade with all the "gold-rich lands of the interior which undoubtedly lined the Niger's banks," according to a report by the African Association.

Finally, it was Mungo Park's turn to plunge into Africa.

In September 1794, Park had appeared at the London offices of the African Association to volunteer his services. He was simply seeking adventure. But the objectives of the backers of the African Association were more serious. Park later wrote about this distinction:

> I had the passionate desire to examine into the productions of a country so little known, and to become experimentally acquainted with the modes of life and character of the natives. . . . The salary which the committee allowed me was sufficiently large, and I made no stipulation for future reward. If I should perish in my journey, I was willing that my hopes and expectations should perish with me; and if I should succeed in rendering the geography of Africa more familiar to my countrymen, and in opening to their ambition and industry new sources of wealth and new channels of commerce, I knew that I was in the hands of men of honour, who would not fail to bestow that remuneration which my successful services should appear to them to merit.

The African Association wanted Park to accompany the consul, James Willis, to Senegambia and then continue on to locate and traverse the Niger River to Timbuktu. That plan, however, changed when bureaucratic and logistical problems combined to delay Willis's departure. Eventually, the British government rescinded Willis's appointment.

Unwilling to wait any longer, Park set out on May 22, 1795, from Portsmouth, on the south coast of England. He was aboard the trade ship *Endeavour*, which in addition to his crew carried a cargo of beeswax and ivory to be traded at the villages and posts along the Gambia.

Park had little idea of the peoples or of the country he would have to pass through to accomplish his mission. When he arrived on the west coast of Africa on June 21, it was the rainy season; almost immediately he caught one of the violent fevers that have always plagued African explorers. But he bore it and survived, using the six months' delay to learn the native language. He stayed in the house of Dr. John Laidley, an Englishman and long-established slave trader who had resided there for many years. The "company and conversation" of his host, wrote Park, "beguiled the tedious hours during that gloomy season when the rain falls in torrents, when suffocating heats oppress by day, and when the night is spent by the terrified traveler in listening to the croaking of frogs (of which the numbers are beyond imagination), the shrill cry of the jackal, and the deep howling of the hyena - a dismal concert, interrupted only by the roar of such tremendous thunder as no person can form a conception of but those who have heard it."

At Pisania, Park also observed the species of flora

and fauna that were unique to this region, and the various "productions of the country" that might make useful trade. He saw alligators and hippopotamuses (or "river-horse"), which he noted "might with more propriety be called the river-elephant, being of enormous and unwieldy bulk, and its teeth furnish good ivory." The Gambia River was abundant with fish – "some species of which are excellent food; but none of them that I recollect are known in Europe" – and sharks, near where it connects to the Atlantic Ocean. As far as trade goods, the natives here cultivated:

Indian corn, onions, yams, cassava, ground nuts, pompions (pumpkins), gourds, watermelons, and some other succulent plants . . .

Cotton and indigo . . . the former of these articles supplies them with clothing, and with the latter, they dye their cloth of an excellent blue colour.

Then, of course, there was the slave trade - Africa's richest and vilest profession. Slaves, Park wrote, were the chief article of trade, though "the whole number which at this time are annually exported from the Gambia, by all nations, is supposed to be under one thousand." He later would note that of all the natives he met on his expedition into the continent's interior, "three-fourths are in a state of hopeless and hereditary slavery and are employed in cultivating the land, in the care of the cattle, and in servile offices of all kinds."

The remarkable journey that Park took from Pisania to the banks of the Niger began on December 2, 1795. He timed his departure to coincide with the "dry season" when the Gambia River "had sunk to its former level, and the tide ebbed and flowed as usual." This, he reckoned, was "the most proper season for traveling, [for] the natives had completed their harvest, and provisions were everywhere cheap and plentiful."

Park pushed into the interior from the mouth of the Gambia with a "coffle," or caravan, of two servants, one horse, and two donkeys. The two servants were native Africans, hired as interpreters and guides. One was a freed slave, called Johnson, who had lived for some years in England; the other was a boy named Demba, who was promised his freedom at the journey's end. Six other travelers accompanied him, two of whom were slave traders.

He had been instructed by his employers in the African Association to carry very little with him; other travelers in Africa had been killed for their possessions. In addition to the small assortment of beads, amber, and tobacco that Park carried for gifts and for trading purposes, he had provisions for only two days and a little money. Among his other scant possessions were a pocket sextant, a compass, a thermometer, two rifles, two pairs of pistols, and an umbrella. He was eventually to be stripped of everything but his horse and his compass.

The first stage of the journey was relatively easy. Park's little expedition went safely among the black tribes who lived between the Atlantic coast and the Niger River just below the Sahara desert. The countryside was thickly wooded brushland, rising gently here and there to ledges of red ironstone and falling back to fertile valleys. Aside from the heat, there was nothing outwardly savage about the landscape. There were wild animals, of course, but the chief danger lay simply in being at the mercy of the tribesmen - many of whom had recently been converted to Mohammedanism. The others, he wrote, "both free and enslaved, persevere in maintaining the blind but harmless superstitions of their ancestors, and are called by the Mahomedans 'kafirs,' or infidels."

Religious or not, the natives were totally indifferent to the travelers' hunger and thirst.

Early in the expedition, Park met local chiefs who were willing to offer up provisions and prayers, in exchange for the rum and other gifts brought from England and the Pisania trading post. He and the other members of his caravan were bestowed with charms and amulets – some no more than scraps of paper marked with passages from the Koran. "Some of the Negroes wear them to guard themselves against the bite of snakes and alligators," Park wrote.

". . . Others have recourse to them in time of war to protect their persons against hostile weapons, but the common use to which these amulets are applied is to prevent or cure bodily diseases, to preserve from hunger and thirst, and generally to conciliate the favour of superior powers under all circumstances and occurrences of life."

But with these tribes, Park soon discovered, nothing ever came free. One afternoon, riding ahead alone in the kingdom of Walli, he was rushed by a group of natives who demanded he pay customs to their king. "I endeavoured to make them comprehend that the object of my journey not being traffic, I ought not to be subjected to a tax like the . . . other merchants who travel for gain," he wrote. "But I reasoned to no purpose. They said it was usual for travelers of all descriptions to make a present to the King of Walli, and without doing so, I could not be permitted to proceed." Park paid for his passage with four bars of tobacco, which seemed to please the natives.

Then, when the expedition had been on the move for nearly a month, it was waylaid by the warriors of a tribal chieftain. They robbed Park of half of his scant goods, claiming that he had tried to slip away without paying the fee that was due their chief. "I had indeed entered the king's frontier, without knowing that I was to pay the duties beforehand," Park wrote, "but I was ready to pay them now, which I thought was all that they could reasonably demand. I then tendered them, as a present to the king, the half ounce of gold which the King of Bondou had given me; this they accepted, but insisted on examining my baggage, which I opposed in vain. The bundles were opened, but the men were much disappointed in not finding in them so much gold and amber as they expected; they made up the deficiency, however, by taking whatever they fancied."

Both servants urged the young Scotsman to turn back. They were being sensible, not cowardly; they saw that Park, whose money was running out, did not have the resources, the experience, or the natural ability to break through the obstacles of African travel.

Park, however, was encouraged by the kindness of an old slave woman who, upon being told that the explorers had been robbed, offered some ground nuts from the basket she carried on her head. "This trifling circumstance gave me peculiar satisfaction," Park wrote. "I reflected with pleasure on the conduct on this poor untutored slave who, without examining into my character or circumstances, listened implicitly to the dictates of her own heart. Experience had taught her that hunger was painful, and her own distresses made her commiserate those of others."

Still, the little party began to live with the constant

threat of starvation. And when they finally came into more friendly territory, the local ruler merely entertained them until he had a well-calculated idea of how much he could take. Having demanded and been given most of Park's remaining goods, the ruler sent him on his way.

Also, the threat of war was in the air. The village drums beat martial tempos; horns were blown as bands of horse-mounted warriors assembled; and the normal, delicately balanced system of bribery and terror that united the tribes was giving way. Park was told on February 12, when he arrived in the territory of Kaarta that he was just in time for the outbreak of hostilities.

The throne of the king of Kaarta was crude - a mound of earth with a leopard skin flung over it - but his words were kindly. He, too, suggested that Park go back. If the king survived the war, which he estimated would take from three to four months, he said he would be glad to receive the explorer as a guest again and send him on toward the great river. In any case, he warned that if Park tried to cross from Kaarta into the territory of the enemy, he would surely be taken for a spy and killed. The only possible route, if he insisted on proceeding, was north around the battle zone and then back to the Niger at Ségou - though this was also dangerous. Why did he go on? Park explained in his journal: "This advice was certainly well meant on the part of the king; and perhaps I was to blame in not following it, but I reflected that the hot months were approaching; and I dreaded the thoughts of spending the rainy season in the interior of Africa. These considerations, and the aversion I felt at the idea of returning without having made a greater progress in discovery, made me determine to go forwards."

The next day, Park sent the king his pistols and his holsters as a gift and then headed northeast into the dry bushland bordering the Sahara. At first, his party grew considerably. The king had granted his request for a guide to take him part of the way, and also provided a retinue of about 200 horsemen. All but two of the king's men turned back when the party reached the village of Toorda on February 14. Two days later, Park and his men found themselves in the middle of a fight.

The explorers had come to a town called Funingkedy, which just before their arrival had been raided and robbed by nomadic Muslims, whom Park referred to as Moors. The bandits had taken advantage of the fact that many of the townspeople had gone to Jarra – a larger town, outside the warring territories – to seek refuge for their families. Park and his party, at first, were mistaken for bandits themselves. Then, he was told that the Moors would come back to take more. On the night of February 16, they did just that.

Park was awakened in the middle of the night by

the screams of women. From the roof of a hut, he watched as five Moors on horseback, firing muskets, absconded with sixteen cattle. Though the townspeople outnumbered the Moors 100 to one, they put up almost no resistance. One boy, who had been guarding the herd, attempted to hurl a spear at the bandits, and for his trouble, was shot in the leg. The boy's mother pleaded with Park, the surgeon, to save him. But there was not much that he could do. As he described it: "I found that the ball had passed quite through his leg, having fractured both bones a little below the knee. The poor boy was faint from the loss of blood, and his situation withal so very precarious, that I could not console his relations with any great hopes of his recovery. However, to give him a possible chance, I observed to them that it was necessary to cut off his leg above the knee. This proposal made everyone start with horror; they had never heard of such a method of cure, and would by no means give their consent to it; indeed, they evidently considered me as a sort of cannibal for proposing so cruel and unheard of an operation, which, in their opinion, would be attended with more pain and danger than the wound itself. The patient was therefore committed to the care of some old Bushreens, who endeavoured to secure him a passage into paradise, by whispering in his ear some Arabic sentences, and desiring him to repeat them. After many unsuccessful attempts . . . the disciples of the

Prophet assured his mother that her son had given sufficient evidence of his faith, and would be happy in a future state. He died the same evening."

To avoid the bandits, it became necessary for Park's party – which numbered about thirty - to travel by night. Doing so, they encountered no more problems on the way to Jarra, which they entered about noon on February 18.

It was near here, the natives told Park, that his predecessor, Major Daniel Houghton, had perished and his body left to rot. That, along with "the difficulties we had already encountered, the unsettled state of the country, and, above all, the savage and overbearing deportment of the Moors," wrote Park, "had so completely frightened my attendants that they declared they would rather relinquish every claim to reward than proceed one step farther to the eastward." Park could not deny the constant danger that they faced of being seized by the Moors and sold into slavery, or killed. So he allowed them to quit the expedition.

Now only one servant, the boy Demba, accompanied him - the other, Johnson, had started back to the Gambia with the explorer's papers. "My faithful boy, observing that I was about to proceed without him, resolved to accompany me," Park wrote, "and told me that though he wished me to turn back, he never had entertained any serious thoughts of deserting me."

Park and Demba circled for days, suffering from thirst and harassed by the Moors. Then, as he was about to enter Ségou and was almost within sight of the Niger, Park was taken prisoner by the troops of Ali, the Muslim king of Ludamar.

In his writings, Park reserved his greatest hatred for these near-white Muslims of the southwestern Sahara. Although he passed among many of their tribes safely, he never felt secure. By contrast, he felt much at home in "black" Africa, where he found the people more civilized, unused to wanton cruelty, and frequently generous and kind.

Five days after he was captured, Park was brought into Chief Ali's nomadic encampment. The land here in the north was intensely dry and covered with stunted acacia shrub. It was almost impossible to travel after noon. There was a hot, dry wind, which will split a man's lips in a few hours and dry his eyes until they feel brittle and ready to crack.

In the following days, Park was tormented in a thousand petty ways. When he fell sick with fever, his captors deliberately teased him and tried to make him feel worse. All of his belongings were taken except his compass, which he had buried in the sandy floor of his hut. But during all this time, he was calm and tried to make himself inconspicuous. That, he learned, was the secret of survival. In his memoir, he later wrote:

It is impossible for me to describe the behaviour of a people who study mischief as a science, and exult in the miseries and misfortune of their fellow-creatures. It is sufficient to observe that the rudeness, ferocity, and fanaticism, which distinguish the Moors from the rest of man-kind, found here a proper subject whereon to exercise their propensities. I was a 'stranger,' I was 'unprotected,' and I was a 'Christian;' each of these circumstances is sufficient to drive every spark of humanity from the heart of a Moor; but when all of them, as in my case, were combined in the same person, and a suspicion prevailed withal, that I had come as a 'spy' into the country, the reader will easily imagine that, in such a situation, I had everything to fear. . . .

Never did any period of my life pass away so heavily; from sunrise to sunset was I obliged to suffer, with an unruffled countenance, the insults of the rudest savages on earth.

Three months passed in this manner. At last, when Park had almost given up any hope of being released, he was allowed to accompany Chief Ali to a southern part of the territory. Park hoped it would be easier to escape.

And Park did escape from Ali, with the few belongings that had been returned to him:

two shirts, two pairs of trousers, two pocket handkerchiefs, an upper and an under waistcoat, a hat, a pair of half boots, and a cloak. He counted the items carefully, knowing they might save his life, and tied them in a bundle. Then at daybreak on July 2, he cautiously slipped out of Ali's camp and set out on his ill-fed horse for Ségou. He left behind his faithful servant.

Almost immediately, Park was waylaid on the road by a new band of tribesmen who eventually decided that stealing his cloak was better than killing him or returning him to Ali.

"Turning my horse's head therefore once more towards the east," he wrote, ". . . I congratulated myself on having escaped with my life, though in great distress, from such a horde of barbarians. . . . It is impossible to describe the joy that arose in my mind, when I looked around and concluded that I was out of danger. I felt like one recovered from sickness; I breathed freer; I found unusual lightness in my limbs; even the Desert looked pleasant."

But his elation did not last long.

As Park proceeded through a wooded country, looking vainly for water and food, at last he was so weakened by thirst that he fell to the sand and could not rise. "Here then," he thought ". . . terminate all my hopes of being useful in my day and generation; here must the short span of my life come to an end."

Toward evening, however, a light rain refreshed him, and he determined to begin again.

For almost another month, he stumbled on - always toward the Niger - begging what he could and occasionally buying grain for his pitiful horse with bits of clothing and odd buttons until he came to his goal.

When he finally reached the river and glimpsed the houses and mosques of Ségou across the slowly flowing water, he sat down exhausted in the sand. The explorer later remembered the great sense of accomplishment that washed over him: "I saw with infinite pleasure the great object of my mission, the long sought-for majestic Niger glittering to the morning sun, as broad as the Thames at Westminster, and flowing slowly *to the eastward*. I hastened to the brink, and having drank of the water, lifted up my fervent thanks in prayer to the Great Ruler of all things for having thus far crowned my endeavors with success."

Park still wanted to reach the lost city of gold, Timbuktu. But he knew that now he could only wait until the ruler of Ségou decided whether to block his passage or let him proceed. Without an invitation, he dared not even make the short boat trip across the river to the king's palace.

At the end of the day, a representative from the king came over to Park. He pointed to a distant village and told the Scotsman to stay there and await further orders. There was little indication that the orders would ever come. To the women of the village, the explorer was a pitiful sight; they sang a song about him, which he translated in his journal:

The winds roared, and the rains fell.

The poor white man, faint and weary,

Came and sat under our tree.

He has no mother to bring him milk;

No wife to grind his corn.

Let us pity the white man:

No mother has he . . .

The king, when he finally did agree to see Park, demanded gifts, of which the explorer had none. (He had given the last two brass buttons from his waistcoat to a woman in the village in exchange for shelter.) The king then demanded that Park leave his village immediately. But he showed some compassion by offering Park 5,000 "kowries" – small shells that were a kind of currency among the tribes – to trade for provisions on his journey. And he provided a guide from his village.

Park continued eastward, through villages and towns that were friendly and generous with provisions. Most of the people here were fishermen who used long cotton nets to scoop great numbers of fish from the Niger.

By now, Park's clothes were worn almost to rags. Still traveling by night to avoid trouble with the Moors, he went days without proper rest. Stings from mosquitoes raised blisters on his legs and arms. Soon, he was sick with fever. He continued on to Silla, a large town across the river, where he was further discouraged to learn that the natives spoke a different language that he did not understand; and he no longer had guides or interpreters to help.

After risking his health, his freedom, and his life to accomplish what few other men could, or would, have done, Park now saw that he must turn back within sight of his goal. He wrote about this decision: "

> I was now convinced, by painful experience, that the obstacles to my further progress were insurmountable. The tropical rains were already set in, with all their violence, the rice grounds and swamps were everywhere overflowed, and, in a few days more, traveling of every kind, unless by water, would be completely obstructed. The cowries which remained of the King of Bambarra's present were not sufficient to enable me to hire a canoe for any great distance, and I had but little hopes of subsisting by charity in a country where the Moors have such influence. But above all, I perceived that I

> was advancing more and more within the power of those merciless fanatics. . . .
>
> The prospect either way was gloomy . . . returning to Gambia, a journey on foot of many hundred miles . . . seemed to be the only alternative, for I saw inevitable destruction in attempting to proceed eastward.

His heart was no longer in the adventure. At last, he began the long journey back to the coast.

Park arrived in England almost a year and a half later. There he was astonished to find that he was not considered a failure. The book that he wrote of his travels was eagerly received; his courage was hailed; he was regarded as an explorer.

Park's return coincided with an upsurge of British interest in Africa and things African. Both the merchants, who wanted new markets, and the scholars, who wanted to complete their picture of the world, were eager to push expeditions forward into the continent. News of Park's partially successful trip spread, and attention was focused even more keenly on the eastward-flowing Niger River: It seemed to be the key to Africa's mysterious heart.

So Park, his faith in himself restored, was sent back to continue his quest. He led a government-sponsored expedition that was very different from his first lonely effort. He was given ample funds and was empowered to enlist soldiers from the British West African base of Gambia.

But things went badly from the beginning. Because of delays in England, the fifty-six-man party had to set out as the rainy season was about to begin. Before they reached the Niger on August 19, 1805, all but eleven members of the expedition were dead of fever. Park and the remaining men struggled to build a small boat, and they finally succeeded in launching it. They called their frail craft His Majesty's Schooner *Joliba,* after the river's native name.

As they floated down the river, each new turning brought a new discovery, a new peril. Because the river continued to flow east, but somewhat north, some of the party thought that it *was* the Nile, as the geographers had foretold. Park himself assumed that the river would soon turn south, and they would see it was the Congo.

What happened to them in that autumn of 1805 is still not entirely known. Park's diary, which was brought back by one of his servants, indicated that they drifted north to Timbuktu, then south with the river into the country now named Nigeria. The natives who lived along the river became increasingly hostile, coming out after the explorers in larger and more tumultuous war parties. Then, according to a guide who was put ashore just before Park and his companions disappeared, they were attacked by the river dwellers at a place where the

Niger's banks come close together. When the *Joliba* was about to be overwhelmed, Park and a young lieutenant leaped into the water, taking with them the other two Europeans who were ill. This was the last that was seen of them.

Park's hope was to get the men to safety, even at the risk of his own life. In that final act of courage, he failed. And he failed to navigate the Niger to its mouth. But in the judgment of his contemporaries, Park had proved himself an explorer; his scouting of the river was an important first link in the chain of discovery that Europeans were to stretch across Africa in the nineteenth century.

2
CARAVELS OF
PORTUGAL

Nearly four centuries before Mungo Park
set off for the Niger, two inquisitive
Portuguese diplomats visited the North
African city of Ceuta. The year was 1413, and the
story they gave out was that they were bound for
Sicily to arrange a marriage between the Sicilian
queen and the second son of their master, the king
of Portugal. The inhabitants of Ceuta, the Moors
- whose language was Arabic but whose racial
lineage was uncertain - let the visitors roam about
the city in peace. Eventually, the Portuguese ship
sailed off again into the Mediterranean.

The Moors would have done well to ask themselves
why the queen of Sicily would consider marrying
a prince who was not the direct heir to the throne

of Portugal. She would not; the diplomatic journey was a hoax. The real purpose of the visitors was to make a report on the defenses of the city to their king, John I, who was considering launching an invasion from Portugal across into Africa.

The two Portuguese spies were African explorers of a sort, though their adventure was totally unlike that of Mungo Park on the Niger River. Indeed, there were many journeys to and through Africa long before the geography of the continent captured the imagination of nineteenth-century Europe. But many of these early voyages were undertaken in secret; they were far removed from each other in time and in country of origin, and few of the maps resulting from them were of much help to later explorers.

On most medieval maps of Africa, the Mediterranean shore was plotted fairly accurately. But, beyond that, the coast was shown as a vague and wandering line between a few known points, and the interior of the continent was filled with pictures of mythical kings and fantastic creatures.

Long before Christ, the ancient Egyptians built a nation that had the strength and imagination to expand beyond the confines of the Nile Valley. An Egyptian mariner who left a record of his voyage on a stone tablet - which would be more helpful if it contained his name and the date of the voyage - sailed down the Red Sea to the coast of what is now Somalia. And there exists a subsequent report of an expedition organized by Pharaoh Necho II and manned by Phoenician sailors that supposedly circumnavigated the continent about 600 BCE. But the Egyptians, for all their love of their own land and its ever-flowing river, had no enduring interest in the extent or the shape of Africa.

The outline of the African continent would not become known until a race of seamen appeared who had the boldness and the technical ability to follow the route of the ancient pharaoh's legendary expedition around Africa.

These sailor-explorers were the fifteenth-century Portuguese, and their leader was Prince Henry, who first took an interest in Africa when he and his brother devised the plan of winning their knighthood by attacking Ceuta. Henry, who was still just a teenager in 1413, claimed that his primary motivation for the siege was to discover the lands beyond Cape Bojador, on the African coast, according to Gomes Eanes de Zurara, Portuguese chronicler and friend to the prince. Zurara's *Chronicle of the Capture of Ceuta* offered rare insight into the early life and conquests of Henry, who much later would become known as "The Navigator" for his role in initiating the Age of Discovery. He described the young prince as: ". . . of a good height and broad frame, big and strong of limb, the hair of his head somewhat erect, his colour naturally fair, but by constant toil and exposure it had become dark. His expression at first sight inspired fear in those who did not know him and when wroth, though such times were rare, his countenance was harsh. He possessed strength of heart and keenness of mind to a very excellent degree, and he was beyond comparison ambitious of achieving great and lofty deeds. . . ."

Indeed, Henry saw the conquest of Ceuta as not only a mission of discovery but also a religious crusade. According to Zurara, he had "learned to hate the infidel in his mother's womb," and now he sought to purge the Muslim influence in the infidel city of Ceuta and spread Christianity to the new lands.

To achieve the latter, Henry sought an ally – the fabled king Prester John, who legend had it, ruled over a Christian nation lost amid the Muslims and pagans. Many, at first, had imagined Prester John's kingdom to be in India, but the Portuguese believed he was in Africa – south of the Sahara Desert and beyond the source of the Nile River. Henry quickly recognized that an alliance with Prester John could reunite East and West, both militarily and spiritually. He thought, according to Zurara, "that if there chanced to be in those lands some population of Christians, or some havens, into which it would be possible to sail without peril, many kinds of merchandise might be brought to this realm, which would find a ready market . . . and also the products of this realm might be taken there, which traffic would bring great profit to our countrymen."

In converting the Moorish Ceuta to Christianity, Henry and his brother would honor the traditions of his family and country – and earn the respect of their father King John and the rewards of wealth and title that came with it.

The princes' first problem was to persuade their father that the attack could succeed.

The reports the two spies had brought back to King John differed completely, yet the king found both of them encouraging.

At first, King John had been skeptical, suspecting that his sons' plan to attack the Moorish city was but youthful foolhardiness. The Moors were reputed to be able fighters, and almost nothing was known of their country. A century and a half before, Christians had tried to capture the North African city of Tunis from its Muslim rulers in an ill-fated campaign that came to be called the Eighth Crusade. But King John was as ambitious as his sons, and he was willing to listen to the men who had seen Ceuta with their own eyes.

The first of them, Captain Alfonso Furtado, said that military considerations were unimportant - as were his own impressions of the fortifications. Much more important, he believed, was the fact that years before on the African coast he had met an old man who told him that a king of Spain or Portugal would be the first monarch to win possessions in Africa. It was clear to Captain Furtado, in a mystical way that made sense to men of the Middle Ages, that this new crusade had been preordained by God.

Heartened but unconvinced, the king then turned to the second voyager, who called for "two sacks of sand, a roll of ribbon, a half-bushel of beans, and a basin." Then, before the king's astonished eyes, he proceeded to make a three-dimensional model of Ceuta. This was very convincing; it seemed obvious from the model that the city could be taken.

King John ordered a survey of his galleys and flatboats. But he also ordered that plans for the invasion proceed with the utmost secrecy. He knew that if word of the impending invasion reached the Moors, they would mobilize the vast numbers of men at their command - tribesmen from the unknown southern reaches of the continent - and Ceuta would be made impregnable. The secret was kept.

The Portuguese fleet arrived in the Strait of Gibraltar in August 1415. As the ships came within sight of Ceuta, the Moors were taken completely by surprise. But they were spared the terror of a lightning assault because the wind blew most of the Portuguese fleet right past the city and into the Mediterranean. There was time to close the gates of the city, and the inhabitants climbed up on the walls to get a better view of the enemy. What they saw - the ships being swept down the coast - made them think they had been saved. So they dismissed the troops that had been hastily called up from the interior when the Portuguese first appeared.

Four days later, the Moors paid for their overconfidence when the invasion fleet returned and drew up along the shore. A Portuguese squire who could not bear to wait any longer jumped into a landing craft and ordered the rowers to take him in. Prince Henry followed, commanding the trumpeters to sound the attack. Five hundred Portuguese stormed onto the beach, and after a fierce struggle pushed the Moors back to the gates of the city. Prince Henry, who had led the attack, held up his men until reinforcements could arrive from the ships. He and his brother agreed that the combined force should then be split up: Henry would press forward with the frontal assault on the city, and his brother would seize the heights commanding Ceuta on the landward side.

Prince Henry then charged once more at the city, and his rush carried him through a gate into the main street. There the tightly packed men hacked away at the Moors with their halberds and swords but could not drive them farther back. At one point, having gained the upper hand, the Moors threatened to rout the Portuguese, and Henry found himself almost alone in a sea of enemy fighters. The chronicler Zurara described the moment vividly. He wrote that Henry, who "was then but twenty-one years of age and whose limbs were vigorous and his courage very great . . . was overcome with rage, and running on the Moors assailed them so strongly that . . . he scattered them."

The Moors retreated to the citadel, the city's stronghold. When Prince Henry reached its gate, he had only seventeen knights and attendants left. Of these, four survived the furious fighting that continued for the next two-and-a-half hours. Henry was finally persuaded to give up the battle and join his brother, who had succeeded in taking the city's mosque. There they spent the night, planning the next day's attack. But when a guard detachment reported that there was no sound from the citadel - a flock of sparrows was resting there quietly, undisturbed by any inhabitants - the two men knew there was no need to fight further. Ceuta belonged to Portugal; it was the first foothold to be gained in Africa by Europeans since the days of Roman conquest.

Prince Henry earned his knighthood as a result of the successful invasion. It was also in Ceuta that he became forever smitten with a fascination for Africa. His imagination was fired by what he saw in the bazaars and storehouses - wares from the East brought overland across the desert. And, undoubtedly, in Ceuta Henry heard more about the Christian kingdom on the other side of the desert, the domain of the legendary Prester John.

The stories told about Prester John were that he was boundlessly rich and powerful. Inspired by these tales, Prince Henry, the newly appointed governor of Ceuta, developed a master plan: He would explore the coasts of Africa until he found a way to the land of Prester John; then their combined forces would outflank the Muslim countries on the Mediterranean and win total victory over the infidels. This scheme of discovery and conquest seemed more important to Henry than any of his other duties. In 1419, he left the royal palace and retired to a lonely promontory called Sagres, on the southern tip of Portugal. There, in his little fortress, he studied and planned; in the process, he created the world's first academy of navigation.

The seafarers sent out from Portugal as a result of Prince Henry's plan sailed in new vessels called caravels, which represented a great improvement over the old fishing smacks, or *barcas,* in which the Portuguese had already voyaged far into the Atlantic. The *barcas* had one stubby mast on which was hung a square sail that allowed them to go only before the wind. But the graceful caravels that Henry's shipbuilders were now constructing had two or three masts with newly designed sails and rigging that allowed them to maneuver far more freely. And the men themselves were as vital to Henry's scheme as were ships and improved navigation instruments. Experienced, adventuresome, and eager to carry their cross and their flag to the ends of the earth, the Portuguese mariners responded brilliantly to their prince's challenge.

In 1418, the Madeira island group was sighted, and in 1432, the Azores were found by Gonçalo Velho Cabral. Two years later, the fearsome Cape Bojador, with its strong currents and prevailing northeasterly winds, was rounded by Gil Eanes, Prince Henry's squire.

Before that time, Cape Bojador (or "the Bulging Cape," which juts into the Atlantic Ocean from the west coast of Africa) had been considered a point of no return. Other sailors had tried and failed to discover what lay beyond it. "Being satisfied of the peril, and seeing no hope of honour or profit, they left off the attempt," wrote Zurara. "For, said the mariners, this much is clear, that beyond this Cape there is no race of men nor place of inhabitants: nor is the land less sandy than the deserts of Libya, where there is no water, no tree, no green herb – and the sea so shallow that a whole league from land it is only a fathom deep, while the currents are so terrible that no ship having once passed the Cape will ever be able to return."

Eanes himself had given up his first expedition, the year before, to round the Cape. He had been intimidated by the stories told about it and excused his failure by recounting the dangers to Prince Henry. But Henry had demanded that his squire try again. "You cannot find a peril so great that the hope of reward will not be greater," Henry said. If Eanes's expedition achieved nothing more than passing the Cape, he said, that would be enough.

Thus encouraged, Eanes sailed fifty leagues beyond Cape Bojador. There seemed to be nothing to force him to stop there; he merely had done what was asked of him. He "found the land without dwellings, but shewing footmarks of men and camels," wrote the chronicler Zurara. Then, in 1434, he came back to Sagres with the reassuring news that the coastline and the sea beyond Cape Bojador were no more formidable than the waters they had always known. He brought, as proof of his discovery, some wild roses.

The greatest prize, of course, was that the barriers of both geography and the imagination finally had been broken. Before Prince Henry died in 1460, reports were brought back that the coast of Africa was, indeed, turning eastward toward the Orient, just as the Prince had hoped. He died believing that his captains had won a whole new continent for Portugal and were on their way to join Prester John.

It was not until 1493, when Pedro da Covilhã crossed the Red Sea from Arabia into Ethiopia, that the kingdom of Prester John was reached.

But five years before that, in 1488, Bartholomeu Dias discovered Africa's southernmost tip. Dias succeeded in this great feat by sailing around the bulge of West Africa into the gulf where the Niger's waters finally emerge, and down the coast past the mouth of the Congo. Then a great storm seized his two vessels and carried them south, out of sight of land, for thirteen days. At last, the storm subsided, and Dias turned east. But there was no land. In hope and wonder, he changed his course to north and finally landed at Mossel Bay. Dias wanted to continue sailing northeastward, but his fearful men forced him to return to Portugal.

When Dias appeared at court, he asserted that one could sail around Africa and beyond. But that honor - the first eastward passage past the Cape of Good Hope and northward along the coast of East Africa - went to Vasco da Gama.

Da Gama was the son of a knight who had served Prince Ferdinand, Duke of Viseu and a cousin of Henry the Navigator. He, like his father, had risen through the ranks of the military Order of Santiago, under Portugal's King John II. Da Gama had done much to help John II's mission to build up the royal treasury – including, in 1492, seizing French ships in retaliation for peacetime attacks on Portuguese shipping. During his reign, John II had greatly expanded the gold and slave trade in West Africa, but he believed greater wealth could be had by discovering a route around Africa to India. It was King John II who had dispatched Covilhã and Dias to scout the trade routes, but it was his successor who would reap the rewards.

The voyage of da Gama was authorized by King Manuel the Fortunate, who like John II had a rather different objective from their cousin Henry. Manuel was interested only in India, which he considered to be the world's greatest source of wealth. He instructed his captains to intensify their African explorations, for he certainly would not reject whatever riches that continent might yield; but he made it clear that the major purpose of voyaging south and east was to reach the Orient. Then Portugal, if it got there first, would command the vital sea route and be the most powerful nation in Europe.

Fortunately, a diary survives of da Gama's amazing journey to India in 1497 - although the Portuguese were not much better as record keepers than the Egyptians. The diary was of interest to later African explorers mainly because of its description of the coastal peoples and its warning of the ever-present possibility of sudden death on a distant shore.

Da Gama sailed on July 8, 1497, from Lisbon with a fleet of four ships and a crew of 170. After sailing for four months, they entered St. Helena Bay, which lies just north of present-day Cape Town on the west coast of Africa. "In this land the men are swarthy," da Gama's diary noted. "They eat only sea wolves and whales and the flesh of gazelles and the roots of plants. . . . They have many dogs like those of Portugal and they bark the same as they do." A while later, the men were attacked by the natives - one of the many sad and bloody encounters between Africans and Europeans.

Da Gama resumed his voyage and rounded the Cape of Good Hope, entering Mossel Bay, where Dias had been before him. Here on the beach, the men erected a stone pillar with a cross on it, the symbol of Christianity and Portuguese sovereignty. But just as they were raising their sails to head northeastward, they saw a band of natives come out from the forest and knock the pillar over. Africa would not be conquered that easily or in that generation.

As they followed the coast into the Indian Ocean, da Gama's men relied, when they could, on native pilots to guide them and to prepare them for new dangers. By the middle of December 1497, the expedition was "already beyond the last discovery made by Bartholomew Dias," da Gama noted in his journal. Still, he found more and more signs that other men in swift ships had been there before him. These were Arabs, who had long held a trade monopoly in the area. When Mozambique's broad harbor was reached, the Portuguese were treated hospitably only because the natives assumed they must be Muslims, too.

When that hospitality inevitably ran out, da Gama and his men took what they wanted by force. One Moor sneeringly suggested that if the Portuguese wanted water, they should go in search of it elsewhere. "We forthwith armed our boats . . . and started for the village," da Gama wrote. A bombardment followed, which the captain described in his journal: "The Moors had constructed palisades by lashing planks together, so that those behind them could not be seen. They were at the time walking along the beach, armed with assegais, swords, bows, and slings, with which they hurled stones at us. But our bombards soon made it so hot for them that they fled behind their palisades . . . this turned out to their injury rather than their profit. During the three hours that we were occupied in this manner, we saw two men killed, one on the beach and the other behind the palisades. When we were weary of this work we retired to our ships to dine."

Along with whatever provisions they could find, the Portuguese took prisoners, some to serve as pilots, or navigators, to the expedition.

From Mozambique, the voyagers sailed for Mombasa, on the coast of Kenya. On the way, they had a pitched battle with another band of Muslim traders who attacked the Portuguese when they drew into a small bay for water. Da Gama fought off the Muslims with the aid of the ships' cannons, killing several and capturing two laden canoes. This fight was not caused by simple hostility or misunderstanding, as before. There was altogether too much understanding on both sides: If Vasco da Gama succeeded in establishing a trade route, Christianity would outflank Islam, and the Arab trade monopoly would be broken.

Da Gama and his men were now eager to complete the final part of their journey to India, the passage across the Arabian Sea. The southwest monsoon was about to set in, and it would take them straight to their goal. At last, in the town of Malindi, just one day's sail northeast of Mombasa.

Vasco da Gama, carrying out Prince Henry's design, had succeeded in charting large sections of the African coast. Henceforth the outlines of the continent would be known, and new explorers could dream of unlocking its interior secrets.

3
CONQUEST OF
THE NIGER

The achievements of such men as Vasco da Gama, and the size and strength of his country's merchant fleet, won for Portugal the mastery of the seas around Africa. Portuguese dominance was threatened for the first time in 1553 when English merchants sailed to Morocco to barter cloth for ivory, gold, and pepper. But it was the Dutch, plunging into the African slave trade, who swept away the Portuguese monopoly of Africa late in the sixteenth century. Then, little more than a century later, the English finally emerged as the supreme foreign power in Africa. Victorious in 1815, at the close of the Napoleonic Wars, Great Britain was free to focus her attention on the vast unexplored regions of the Dark Continent.

By this time, Mungo Park had already gone to Africa and had died while seeking the mouth of the Niger. Now the British proposed sending other expeditions to Africa to try and follow the river's course. In 1822, a government-sponsored expedition set out for Tripoli: Guiding it were a naval lieutenant named Hugh Clapperton and Major Dixon Denham.

Clapperton at thirteen had apprenticed aboard a merchant ship that traded between England and North America. After making several trips across the Atlantic Ocean, he joined the Royal Navy, serving honorably during the Napoleonic Wars against France. On a visit home to Scotland, he met a physician, Walter Oudney, who first sparked his interest in Africa.

Oudney had been appointed by the British government as consul, to promote trade to the sub-Saharan kingdom of Bornu (present-day Nigeria). Others before him had tried to reach Bornu and failed. Oudney hoped he would have better luck with Clapperton escorting him. In early 1822, they set out south from Tripoli to Murzuk, where they were joined by Dixon Denham.

A friend once wrote of Denham, "He was the kind of man who must have adventure or he rots." The son of a London haberdasher, he had joined the army at twenty-five. He was distinguished for bravery during the Napoleonic Wars.

Intrigued by tales of African explorations, Denham decided to follow Clapperton. When Denham caught up to the expedition at Murzuk, he found Clapperton and Oudney in a miserable state; the first suffering from fever, and the latter from a severe cold. Denham soon learned, too, that the expedition had been detained by a local bey, or chieftain, who refused to let it proceed while he was away on a slave-raiding mission. To enforce this restriction, the tribe took the explorers' camels. Known to have a mean streak, the domineering Denham lashed out angrily at his new partners, Clapperton and Oudney. Then, he turned back toward Tripoli to seek more funds, as well as an escort, from the bashaw, or governor of the region.

After Dixon left, Clapperton wrote to Sir John Barrow, a friend and sponsor of the expedition: "His absence will be no loss to the Mission, and a saving to his country, for Major Denham could not read his sextant, knew not a star in the heavens, and could not take the altitude of the sun." Oudney later wrote a letter to the British consul in Tripoli, comparing Denham to a snake hidden in the grass. Denham fired back his own accusations, calling Oudney and Clapperton incompetent. He went as far as to ask Lord Bathurst, the expedition's chief sponsor, to promote him to commander in place of Oudney.

It was September of 1822 before Denham made

his way back to Murzuk. Finally, he had come to an agreement with the bashaw that allowed the explorers – for a hefty price - to join the 300-man escort of a merchant headed to Bornu. Besides Denham, Clapperton, and Oudney, the party included a fourth Englishman (a carpenter named Hillman), five servants, and four camel drivers. They departed from Murzuk on November 18, 1822.

The course they followed took them across the Sahara and through the plains and grassy steppes of the Sudan. The perils of desert travel were many - not the least of them being the expected shortage of water. The men sometimes traveled three days without finding a well, stepping over the dried carcasses of men and animals that had preceded them and perished from thirst and fatigue.

And there were sandstorms, too - so violent, Major Denham wrote, "as to fill the atmosphere and render the immense space before us impenetrable to the eye beyond a few yards." But they let nothing stop them. The Niger was their goal, and having come a great distance already, they could not bring themselves to turn back.

Their first target was not the Niger itself, but Lake Chad that had long been thought to have some connection with the Niger. Perhaps the lake was the place where the Niger and Congo rivers met, for many people believed these rivers to be one and the same. Or perhaps the lake was the gateway to the rich cities that were believed to be strung out like pearls along Africa's water courses.

The expedition finally reached the lake in February 1823 after traveling more than 1,000 miles overland, which in itself was an extraordinary accomplishment. Denham wrote that upon seeing Lake Chad, "My heart bounded within me . . . for I believed this lake to be the great object of our search."

Denham was destined for disappointment because Lake Chad proved to have no connection with the Niger or with any of Africa's major river systems. However, since they were the first Europeans to have seen this body of water, they could take comfort in having made an important discovery.

The expedition was now in Bornu, a province of modern Nigeria, and on a March morning in 1823, the men were summoned for an audience with the region's portly sultan. According to Denham, they arrived in the sultan's court and saw his many subjects seated in a huge semicircle around his cagelike pavilion "with their backs to his royal person."

"Large bellies and large heads are indispensable for those who serve the court of Bornu," Denham wrote. And to meet these requirements, the natives padded their stomachs with wadding and wrapped their heads in enormous turbans of muslin or linen. "Nothing could be more ridiculous than the appearance of these people squatting down in their places, tottering under the weight and magnitude of their turbans and their bellies while the thin legs that appeared underneath but ill accorded with the bulk of the other parts."

Soon after visiting the sultan, the expedition split up. Clapperton, Oudney, and some of the men set off toward the west, heading for the great Arab trading town of Kano. Denham, on the other hand, joined a group of friendly Bornu tribesmen and went south. It was a foolish move because Denham quickly became involved in a savage skirmish between the natives he accompanied and a host of their enemies.

Denham watched in terror as enemy warriors literally butchered some of the men of his party. The warriors wounded him with their spears, but according to Denham, "They were alone prevented from murdering me ... I am persuaded, by the fear of injuring the value of my clothes, which appeared to them a rich booty." They tore his clothing from him, he recalled, and when they began to fight over it, "the idea of escape came like lightning across my mind, and without a moment's hesitation or reflection I crept underneath the belly of the horse nearest me and started as fast as my legs could carry me for the thickest part of the wood."

He eventually rejoined the tribesmen who had been his companions and continued his journey.

Unable to find the Niger, or any significant body of water, Denham returned north and explored the eastern shore of Lake Chad.

Clapperton's party, meanwhile, had not fared much better. On January 12, 1824, Oudney died of illness in the village of Murmur, near the present-day town of Katagum, Nigeria. Clapperton, himself weakened by a lingering fever, buried his friend there and continued westward. He was determined to reach Kano, however, because he had heard much about it during his travels. The town was the commercial center of the entire region that lay between Lake Chad and the Niger.

Clapperton showed the effects of his illness and of his long overland journey as he halted outside the city. The sun had burned his skin to a dark, brackish hue, and his face appeared wasted and gaunt. He rested under a tree, and after a good night's sleep prepared to enter the city the next day: January 20, 1824. He shed the dusty clothes he had been wearing and arrayed himself in his full-dress naval uniform. His high collar and still-gleaming gold buttons transformed him into a semblance of the strikingly tall, athletic Scotsman he had been at the outset of the journey.

Describing his arrival in Kano, Clapperton wrote: "I had no sooner passed the gates than I felt grievously disappointed, for from the flourishing description of it given by the Arabs, I expected to see a city of surprising grandeur. I found, on the contrary, the houses nearly a quarter of a mile from the walls, and in many parts scattered into detached groups, between large and stagnant pools of water. I might have spared all the pains I had taken . . . for not an individual turned his head round to gaze at me, but all, intent on their own business, allowed me to pass by without notice or remark."

Clapperton could not have known it, but the citizens of Kano were used to seeing costumes far more splendid than his. Every day, traders from the Eastern Sudan, the Gold Coast, and regions as far north as the Mediterranean poured through the gates of the city.

Despite his initial disappointment, the Scotsman developed a liking for Kano. He remained there a full month, enjoying the bustling markets and the ceremonial boxing matches. Then he went on to Sokoto, where he boldly initiated conversations with Sultan Bello, one of the most influential rulers of West Africa.

At first, the talks with the sultan went well because Clapperton was both a good talker and a good listener. But at the second meeting, he made the mistake of saying that the people and the government of Britain wished the slave trade to be discontinued. He should have known that the sultan derived most of his income from the capture and sale of slaves and that he would fight to the death any attempt to cut off that important source of revenue. It was perhaps because of Clapperton's unfortunate slip of the tongue that he was not permitted to proceed to the Niger, now only 150 miles away. Disappointed, he turned back and met Denham near Lake Chad. They arrived in England in June 1825, their mission unfulfilled.

The lure of trade with West Africa was too great for the British government to let this failure be a defeat. They were determined to chart the full length of the Niger. Clapperton was promoted to commander and awarded a new expedition to the interior, this time from the coast of West Africa.

Only one of the four men who started out with Clapperton continued on for long, his twenty-one-year-old servant, Richard Lander. Two of the other four died early on and the third went off on his own.

Lander had traveled widely, despite his youth. Since leaving school at the age of thirteen, he had served many masters on voyages to various parts of Europe and to the West Indies and South Africa. And it was Africa, more than any other land, that appealed to his romantic spirit. Sometime later, he would write, "There was a charm in the very sound of 'Africa' that always made my heart flutter on hearing it mentioned."

Clapperton and Lander reached the Niger in the

spring of 1826 and proceeded along the route that Clapperton had tried to follow once before. Gradually they made their way to Kano and then to Sokoto, where Clapperton hoped to reopen discussions with Sultan Bello. Britain was eager to conclude a trade agreement with the powerful ruler, and Clapperton was determined to bring it about.

However, when Clapperton reached the sultan's camp, he found the potentate wholly committed to war and only remotely interested in entering into negotiations with any foreign power. Clapperton resolved to be patient and remain near Sokoto until it was advantageous for him to have a long, and hopefully fruitful, talk with the sultan.

Then on March 12, 1827, Clapperton suffered an attack of dysentery. It was left to Lander to care for him, which proved a supreme test of his loyalty as a servant, and of his devotion. In his journal, Lander wrote: "From the moment he was first taken ill, Captain Clapperton perspired freely, large drops of sweat continually rolling over every part of his body . . . and being unable to obtain anyone, even of our own servants, to assist, I was obliged to wash the clothes, kindle and keep in the fire, and prepare the victuals with my own hands."

On the morning of April 13, Lander awoke to the sound of Clapperton's loud breathing. He saw his master struggling to get to his feet, a wild expression on his face. Lander ran to him. Then, the young servant stated, "I clasped him in my arms, and whilst I thus held him, could feel his heart palpitating violently. His throes became every moment less vehement, and at last they entirely ceased." Clapperton fell back - dead.

Lander's grief did not sway him from his mission. As his master had requested, he retrieved Clapperton's papers and delivered them back to England. He wrote an account of his adventures which was published along with Clapperton's journal in 1829.

But Lander's career in Africa was far from over. He was only twenty-five and a persuasive man despite the humbleness apparent in his writings. Being a servant did not stop him from asking the government to send him to Africa to trace the Niger from Bussa to its mouth.

He finally received backing for his expedition, but it was a paltry amount - only 100 pounds - hardly enough to take care of his needs or those of his brother John, whom he intended to take along. The Landers reached Dahomey on March 22, 1830, and arrived at Bussa on June 17. Three months later, when they had hired some native helpers, they set out on their great adventure down the Niger's sluggish current.

At a village called Bocqua, midway between Bussa and the sea, the brothers and their men left the boats and climbed ashore to rest. But their relaxation was interrupted by one of the men who rushed into camp, screaming in terror that some natives were about to attack them. Richard Lander wrote that he then saw "a large party of men, almost naked, running . . . toward our encampment. They were all variously armed with muskets, bows and arrows, knives, . . . long spears, and other instruments of destruction."

Lander and his men gathered up their muskets and pistols, but he was determined to avoid bloodshed - for one important reason: He knew his party was outnumbered and could neither win a battle with these natives nor escape from them. Lander ordered his men not to fire unless they were fired on first, and the group stood fast.

The natives were advancing swiftly now, and Lander noticed that one of them, who appeared to be the chief, was walking ahead of the others. The Lander brothers threw down their pistols and calmly walked toward him. Richard described the encounter in his journal: "As we approached him we made all the signs and motions we could with our arms to deter him and his people from firing on us. His quiver was dangling at his side, his bow was bent, and an arrow which was pointed at our breasts already trembled on the string when we were within a few yards of his person. This was a highly critical moment - the next might be our last. But the hand of Providence averted the blow, for just as the chief was about to pull the fatal cord, a man that was nearest him rushed forward and stayed his arm. At that instant we stood before him and immediately held forth our hands; all of them trembled like aspen leaves. The chief looked up full in our faces . . . his body was convulsed all over, as though he were enduring the utmost torture . . . he drooped his head, eagerly grasped our proffered hands, and burst into tears. This was a sign of friendship - harmony followed, and war and bloodshed were thought of no more."

The Landers were fortunate that time, but a bit farther downstream, their good fortune ran out. About fifty native canoes were sighted coming toward them; some had the British Union Jack mounted on bamboo poles, and sewed to some other flags were figures of men's legs and of chairs, tables, decanters, and glasses. The people in the canoes were dressed as Europeans except that they did not wear trousers. In that part of the country, only chiefs were allowed to have trousers.

At first, Richard Lander was overjoyed at the sight of these people - until he noticed they were pointing muskets at him. There was no chance to stage a successful fight or to flee. The Lander brothers were seized, their supplies and clothing stolen, and soon they learned that they were to be handed over as prisoners to the ruler of a region nearby. But when they were brought to that ruler's court, they were ransomed by another ruler, named King Boy, who hoped to get an even higher price for the two foreigners at the coast.

But neither of the brothers despaired. They endured their privations patiently, in much the way of Mungo Park. Soon they were brought to the coastal town of Brass, and King Boy proceeded to bargain with the captain of the English brig *Thomas* for custody of John and Richard Lander.

The captain of the brig succeeded in getting both brothers on board and kicking off King Boy without paying him a penny of the promised ransom money. After spending a terrifying time while the vessel tried to sail out across a sand bar - with the natives waiting grimly on the shore for a shipwreck - the Landers felt the salt air in their faces and knew that at last their terrible journey was over. It had been arduous, but it had been a success. The brothers arrived in England with the definite information that the Niger River came down to the sea in the Gulf of Guinea. They had won for their country one of Africa's most sought-after prizes.

4
TO TIMBUKU

Lieutenant Hugh Clapperton, leading an official British expedition, was the first European of his times to cross the Sahara. Others before him died trying. His route on the map looks like the only sensible way for a European to get to West Africa above the Gulf of Guinea: It leads directly south from the Mediterranean port of Tripoli. But, in fact, the route is the most perilous in Africa, as later explorers found.

The Sahara, which stretches completely across North Africa, 3,000 miles from the Atlantic to the Nile, looks from the air like the face of a burned-out planet. But it is by no means dead or featureless. Mountains as lofty as 11,000 feet thrust up from valleys no higher than sea level, and here and there are oases large enough and fertile enough to support sizeable cities. The most commonly held misconception about the world's greatest desert is that it is all sand. Actually the rippled sand dunes, which are found mostly in the region directly below the Atlas Mountains, take up only one-seventh of the Sahara's total area.

Two other parts of the Sahara give a better idea of the great desert's variety - and its hostility. They are the Ahaggar range, which has been called the mountain heart of the Sahara, and the Tanezrouft plain, which has all the beauty of an endless, uninhabited parking lot. In the Ahaggar Mountains live the proudest of the six Tuareg tribes. Here they have been able to keep their strange language and ancient customs unchanged; they retreated here, among these wild gorges and wind-eroded peaks after raiding the rich oases at the desert's fringe. The Tanezrouft has also served as a haven for fugitives - its shale-covered surface is so rough that no foot leaves a trace - but no man by himself can stand its monotonous loneliness for long without going mad.

Yet it was through the Tanezrouft region that René Caillié traveled, the next European after Clapperton to cross the Sahara and live to tell of it. Caillié's goal was Timbuktu. He wanted to be the first Westerner to reach the city whose existence, despite its position as the hub of the Sahara's caravan traffic, was then still only a rumor outside Africa.

Of all the nineteenth-century explorers of Africa, Caillié seemed the least likely to succeed. He was poor, uneducated, skilled in neither science nor language, totally without influence, not robust, and so unprepossessing that he had difficulty commanding an audience even after his great accomplishments were known. The one quality that led him through his adventures was an incredible will to see and to overcome Africa.

Caillié was born in the French village of Mauzé in 1799, the sixth child of an impoverished baker. Even his youth was occupied by thoughts of exploration. "All my spare time," he wrote later, "was taken up with books of travel. The map of Africa, which so far as I could see showed only desert or unexplored regions, fired my imagination above all others." He had been gripped by author Daniel Defoe's adventure novel *Robinson* Crusoe, and even more so by Mungo Park's accounts of his travels in Africa.

By the time he was sixteen, Caillié's imagination was focused on Timbuktu. Determined to reach that legendary ancient city, he set out from his native village with a few personal possessions in his knapsack and sixty francs (about $12) in his pocket.

In 1816, Caillié reached the coast of Africa but not much farther. He joined a British expedition but heat and lack of water forced him to turn back. Three years later he signed onto another expedition and made it as far as Bundu (in present day Senegal) before coming down with malaria.

The determined Frenchman was twenty-five when he came to Africa for the third time. This time he traveled alone and intended to disguise himself as a Muslim, reach Timbuktu by way of the Niger River, then cross the totally unexplored western part of the Sahara to Tangier. Setting off from the coast of Senegal, he walked without stopping until he found a native tribe willing to let him live among them and learn their language. He ate the food, wore the clothes, and endured the hardships of these Arabic-speaking black Bedouins. But their tolerance never reached the point of civility; he was never afforded any privacy. And no matter how often he repeated their Islamic prayers with them or how patiently he bore their rudeness, Caillié was always regarded as a freakish animal. He endured it for a year.

Then, after working an additional year at an English post to earn more money, he started at last for Timbuktu. It was April 19, 1827, when he left the coast. Caillié's determination was reinforced by news that the Geographical Society of Paris had offered a 10,000-franc reward to any Frenchman who succeeded in bringing back a firsthand report from that city. As a precaution, he had prepared a story that he considered believable enough to ensure a friendly reception from natives along the way. He said that he had been born in Egypt of Arab parents and as a baby had been taken to France by Napoleon's army; now he was trying to return to the land of his birth by way of Timbuktu.

Caillié joined a small native caravan heading into the interior, and he was relieved to find that his story was accepted by tribesmen along the route. Apparently his knowledge of Islamic law calmed the suspicions aroused by his white skin. Yet he was pestered and robbed, once by the leader of his own caravan; Caillié made no complaint. He and his companions kept on at a fierce pace - traveling without a break from six in the morning until midafternoon - and thus, they arrived on the upper Niger in less than two months. But it was still some distance to Timbuktu, and the brutality of the journey was beginning to affect the young Frenchman.

The first sign of this was a hideous sore on Caillié's foot; then he became afflicted with scurvy. Finally, the caravan abandoned him, and he underwent "incredible suffering," praying unashamedly for death. But in the hut of a kindly native, he finally recovered and was able to proceed again.

Caillié completed the last 500 miles of his journey on a primitive cargo boat going down the Niger. The Muslims still believed his story and treated him fairly well. However, as he was almost without funds, he was forced to sleep on the open deck and share the food of slaves who were being transported downriver. At dawn on April 20, 1828, he entered Timbuktu. He recorded his first reaction: "I have never felt a similar emotion, and my transport was extreme. I was obliged, however, to restrain my feelings, and to God alone did I confide my joy."

A closer look at the town was a letdown for Caillié. "The city presented . . . nothing but a mass of ill-looking houses built of earth. Nothing was to be seen in all directions but immense plains of quicksand of a yellowish-white color. The sky was a pale red as far as the horizon." On further inspection, Caillié found that some of the inhabitants lived comfortably enough. However, none were free from the threat of violence because the city was constantly menaced by the Tuaregs, masters of the Sahara that stretched beyond the dazzling horizon to the north.

The North African merchants of Timbuktu welcomed Caillié, and he was lodged in a house near the marketplace. But he was miserable, for this was not the city he had yearned to find. After traveling an entire year to get there, he stayed only two weeks.

On May 4, 1828, he left with a caravan of 600 camels and headed across the Western Sahara. His course was much farther west than Clapperton's 1823 route and was roughly parallel to it. Caillié's caravan started into the unrelieved heat and monotony of the Tanezrouft, where several days' journey separated each meager well. Gradually conditions worsened. Once in a sandstorm, blinded and lost, he was sure he would die. But he and the other scattered parts of the great caravan re-formed and started on again. Weeks passed, and the men of the caravan became increasingly hostile. In the middle of the Sahara, they forced Caillié to dismount from his camel. He walked the rest of the way, suffering all the indignities and the privations of a slave. He called the experience - the stonings and beatings and bedevilings - "a martyrdom infinitely worse than death."

After three months of traveling through unmapped desert, Caillié dared strike out on his own when the Atlas Mountains came into sight. But the Moroccan territory that he still had to pass through to reach the port city of Tangier was forbidden to foreigners. A Christian would be killed immediately if he was caught.

Proceeding cautiously by night, Caillié finally reached the Moroccan capital of Fez, where a representative of the French government would not let him hide or rest. The French envoy could not be convinced that this bundle of rags and sunburned skin begging for aid was really a civilized European. So Caillié continued on to the north and made it to Tangier, on the Strait of Gibraltar, on September 7. There he found a consul who recognized him as a European, and who, after hearing the traveler's story, realized the importance of his achievement.

Caillié had covered more than 2,800 miles in 538 days. When he finally returned to Paris, he was received as a hero. He was made a chevalier of the Legion of Honor and was toasted at a special meeting of the Geographical Society of Paris. He claimed, too, his prize of 10,000 francs for being the first European to reach Timbuktu and return to talk about it.

Caillié achieved what he had set out to do, but his health was ruined and his spirit was broken. Laboriously, he completed the report of his journey, which the people of Paris very quickly came to doubt. They, too, had expected more of Timbuktu - and they challenged his description of it. For all his relentless courage, Caillié remained an amateur explorer; he did not have the skill or the temperament to give a scientifically accurate account of what he had seen. Many people began to doubt that he had actually reached Timbuktu. Even the government came to regard him less respectfully, and eventually, it denied him a part of his promised pension. He died in 1838, forgotten and impoverished, at the age of thirty-nine.

It was left to a German - and a wholly different kind of explorer - to salvage Caillié's reputation.

In London in 1850, preparations were being

made to outfit the English Mixed Scientific and Commercial Expedition. After the travels of Clapperton and Caillié, the British recognized the extent and value of the desert territories between the Mediterranean and the Niger. But questions remained about the risks and dangers if they were to control the area. More exploration was needed.

Having only recently returned from Africa, James Richardson was the obvious man to lead this new British effort. His experience reconnoitering the Sahara slave routes for English missionary societies made him uniquely qualified for the assignment. It helped that he had already published two books on his *Travels Into the Great Desert of Sahara*. But Richardson could not find men of sufficient scientific skill or interest in either Britain or France. When he met Dr. Heinrich Barth, a philosopher and geographer of Hamburg, he felt he had found someone as keenly interested in Africa.

The scholarly Dr. Barth soon proved himself to be the ablest man of the expedition, partly because of his tolerance, but also because he had traveled previously in Africa and had some knowledge of Arabic.

Barth's friend German geologist Adolf Overweg also joined the expedition.

The route of the 1850 expedition skirted around the Ahaggar Mountains and passed through a region of which nothing was known in Europe - nothing except that an Arab traveler named Ibn Battuta had been through it in the fourteenth century. Once, Richardson and Barth came upon a caravan of slave traders, all of whom had been murdered by marauding tribesmen from the mountains. Then they, too, were stopped by an onrush of Tuaregs. They were released only after one-third of their goods had been taken; Barth commented merely that the expedition should not have aroused the natives' greed by taking so many supplies.

After crossing the Sahara from north to south, the party reached Lake Chad toward the beginning of 1851. There Richardson died, another victim of Africa's murderous climate. Then, in September 1852, Adolf Overweg became feverish and died, ten miles east of the village of Kuka, near the western shore of Lake Chad.

Left on his own, Barth decided to continue the journey and carry out his mission by adapting himself completely to African ways. He donned the long robes of an Arab and learned the language of the natives in the Chad area. He called himself Abd el Kerim, "Servant of the Lord," but he did not do so to deceive the natives - nor, with his great blond beard, could he have passed as an African. He hoped, rather, to stay among the natives and study them, trying to understand their culture by steeping himself in it.

He wandered through the once-mighty Sudanese

kingdoms near Lake Chad and made his headquarters on the lake's western shore. By his honesty and energy, he even won the respect of the local sultan. His own supplies having long since given out, he lived on the kindness of the sultan of Bornu for several months. At length, in September 1852, a packet from England reached him with a letter recognizing him as head of the expedition and ordering him to proceed to Timbuktu.

In September 1853, Barth reached Timbuktu, more than 1,000 miles west of Lake Chad. Suddenly, he was "seized with a severe attack of fever," and he heard rumors of a plot by a fanatic in the sultan's court to kill him. The chieftain he had paid for protection now was demanding a higher price – most of the trade goods and provisions he carried. Barth did all he could to maintain his disguise as a Muslim; to those who suspected him, he protested loudly that he ascribed to "the pure Islam, the true worship of the one God, dating from the time of Adam, and not from the time of Mohammed."

While he recovered his health and negotiated his safety, he remained confined to a house that offered a limited view of the town.

Eventually, he saw that Timbuktu was essentially as Caillié had claimed. And he vowed that the Frenchman would get the credit for having been there first. However, his reaction to the town differed from his predecessor's. To Barth, Timbuktu was not the drab collection of mud huts that had so depressed Caillié, but an enormously rich storehouse of research possibilities. In his journal, he recorded those impressions:

> On the north was the massive mosque of Sankoré, which had just been restored to all its former grandeur . . . and gave the whole place an imposing character. . . . The style of the buildings was various. I could see clay houses of different characters, some low and unseemly, others rising with a second story in front to greater elevation, and making even an attempt at architectural ornament, the whole being interrupted by a few round huts of matting. . . .
>
> At the same time I became aware of the great inaccuracy which characterizes the view of the town as given by M. Caillié; still, on the whole, the character of the single dwellings was well represented by that traveler, the only error being that in his representation the whole town seems to consist of scattered and quite-isolated houses while in reality the streets are entirely shut in as the dwellings form continuous and uninterrupted rows. But it must be taken into account that Timbuktu at the time of Caillié's visit was not so well off as it is at present . . . and he

had no opportunity of making a drawing on the spot.

When the rumored attack came, instead of fleeing and relinquishing all of his goods as his servants suggested, Barth armed his party and prepared to fight. His supposed protector, seeing this display, asked if he "meant to fight the whole population of the town, uttering the words *'guwet é Rum*,'" which meant "strength of the Christians." Somehow, it worked. "Certainly, for the moment," Barth wrote, "my energetic conduct had dispersed the clouds that might have been impending over my head."

Still, Barth's bravery did not dissuade the natives from "begging for more presents day by day." And his fever came and went – seemingly exacerbated by the almost constant thunderstorms during his stay in Timbuktu. His health declined so drastically that he began to contemplate death. On September 27, he wrote: "This was the anniversary of the death of Mr. Overweg, my last and only European companion, whom I had now outlived a whole year and whom, considering the feeble state of my health at this time, while my mind was oppressed with the greatest anxiety, I was too likely soon to follow to the grave."

Dr. Barth remained in Timbuktu for eight months. During that time, he studied the town's topography, history, economy, foods, customs, conflicts, and people – everything in minute detail. He surveyed and drew maps showing the layout of streets and buildings in relation to natural landmarks. His health and other inconveniences of poor weather and uncooperative natives combined to extend his stay far beyond what he thought was necessary.

Then, late in March of 1854, rival tribes in the region escalated their feuds and he decided to leave, which he did on April 19.

After traveling for ten months on the Niger and overland, Barth reached Lake Chad again in January of 1855. By this time, he was close to starvation; he was diseased, and oppressed by loneliness. But his courage revived when he heard of Europeans in a nearby village. Scarcely believing his eyes when he saw an English and a German flag flying in the distance, he fell into the arms of three white men who came to greet him. The men, led by a young German named Eduard Vogel, had been sent out by the British government to look for Barth. As delighted as they all were to see one another, none of them were particularly surprised to have accomplished such a feat. The age of African exploration was, indeed, advancing to the point where the paths of European explorers might be expected to cross.

Barth returned to Europe by an easterly route through the desert. His five-volume journal, *Travels in Africa,* became mandatory reading for those who journeyed after him - traders, soldiers, and administrators. It not only described Saharan and sub-Saharan Africa with a professional accuracy that adventurers like Park and Caillié could never have achieved but set forth guidelines for safe passage through the continent. Be deliberate, the book urged future explorers, and have the ability to await results patiently.

Years later, when Barth was advising a young protégé who was on the point of leaving for Africa, Barth said, "The best weapon for the Christian traveler in Africa is decency - impeccable decency - toward the natives." If his words had been remembered, the history of African development might not have been as bloodstained and tragic as it was.

5
THE GREAT TREK

The exploration of South Africa had a totally different character from that of any other part of the continent. The region that lies north of the Cape of Good Hope was to be explored and opened up not by isolated and courageous individuals, but by Dutch colonialists.

Though Portuguese explorers and traders had been back and forth around the Cape ever since the end of the fifteenth century, they had little use for the area except as a station for getting fresh supplies of food and water for their ships. Their real interest lay in their colonies on the west and east coasts of Africa and in India.

However, a shipwreck off the Cape of Good Hope

in 1648 led to the establishment of a Dutch colony there four years later.

The 500-ton Dutch cargo ship *Haarlem* was sailing from Batavia to the Netherlands when it was wrecked in Table Bay near the Cape. Despite being the smallest in the fleet of three ships, the *Haarlem* was laden with valuable cargo – pepper, cinnamon, candy sugar, gold cloth, Chinese porcelain, and indigo. Unable to load the cargo onto the other two ships, and unwilling to leave it behind, the captain of the *Haarlem* ordered his crew to stay on the Cape and salvage what they could. Left behind, the crew, now commanded by two junior officers named Leendert Janssen and Nicholas Proot.

The Hollanders wasted no time in building a 450-square-foot temporary fort that they called Sandeburgh, to protect them from the indigenous people – the Khoekhoe ("men of men"), whom they called Hottentots. Displaying great resourcefulness, they collected various vegetable seeds from the wrecked ship, dug up the soil, and raised the crops. They also dug a well, twenty meters deep, from which they could draw fresh water. They hunted penguins and cormorants (large water birds) and bartered with the natives for cattle and sheep. Near their camp, they discovered a salt marsh, which helped with the preservation of food and prevention of scurvy. As a result, the Hollanders not only survived, they thrived.

When another Dutch fleet – twelve ships, under the command of Admiral Wollebrant Geleijnszoon de Jongh – arrived in April 1648, the men at the fort provided the scurvy-stricken crew with fresh meat and vegetables, which was just the cure they needed. The crews of the rescue ships, of course, were surprised – having expected to find men dead, or half-dead, but instead finding them better off than themselves. One of those impressed crewmen was the ship's surgeon Jan van Riebeeck, who would become the first administrator of the future Dutch Colony, Cape Town.

Back in Holland, Janssen and Proot gave a report on their settlement at the Cape of Good Hope, in which they praised the climate, the rich soil, and the rivers that flowed without ceasing. Largely because of their enthusiastic descriptions, the Dutch East India Company sent three ships to the Cape in 1652 under the command of Jan van Riebeeck.

Van Riebeeck was instructed to establish a station that would supply water, vegetables, and meat to company ships en route to and from India. Water was plentiful enough, but food was more difficult to obtain, and from time to time, the Dutch East India Company had to send supplies to the settlers. But gradually, van Riebeeck and his people began to plant gardens, learned to hunt successfully, and even traded with the natives for cattle and sheep. Although the colony was not a complete success as a way station, the settlers had established a foothold on the Cape.

Then, in 1684, more pioneers were sent out from Holland, and shortly afterward, a group of refugees from religious persecution in France arrived at the Cape. Almost all of these settlers, however, became discontented with the rule of the Dutch East India Company. And as the colonists prospered, they began to explore and settle farther inland, where they hoped to find a measure of independence.

This was the start of that tremendous movement in South African history known as trekking, a migration that paralleled in many ways the opening up of the American West. The geography of the two regions was similar, for the inland territories of South Africa were nearly as vast as those of America. From the Cape, it was 1,250 miles to the Zambezi River, and though the sprawling Kalahari Desert occupied the west-central part of the area, there were millions of square miles of uplands that had a temperate climate and were well-suited for farming and cattle raising.

In some districts, grazing land was taken by force from the natives, who also raised cattle, just as the pioneers in America later took land from the Indians. This violence, whites against blacks, was precisely what Barth had warned against. It is often forgotten, however, that many natives themselves were engaged in conquest.

In fact, a great wave of Bantu tribes was advancing from the north at almost the same time as Dutch farmers - called Boers - were moving up from the south. The only long-time inhabitants of this land were the Khoekhoe (Hottentots) and the Bushmen, the nomadic hunters of South Africa.

As in America, riches other than farmland began to attract the settlers. At first, no one suspected the existence of the gold and diamonds that were found later in South Africa. But as early as 1681, tribesmen from the west arrived at the Cape with samples of copper ore dug from a mountain near them. Word began to spread of the easily obtainable mineral riches. In August 1685, the governor of the Cape, Simon van der Stel, decided to lead an expedition to find the source of the ore.

After slogging through swamps and rattling over rocky hills on which a number of their wagons and carts were wrecked, van der Stel and his company reached the Copper Mountains on October 21, 1685. "The mountains were colored from top to bottom with verdigris [copper carbonate]," they noted with joy. The men built smelting furnaces, and at last, after several disappointments, obtained copper.

These pioneers of South Africa were practical explorers who penetrated the interior to find a livelihood for themselves and their families. They were not concerned with the triumphs of discovery; they had come to conquer, and to stay.

The new land was as rich as it was beautiful, and they intended to prosper on it.

At the beginning of the eighteenth century, the Cape colony had a population of about 10,000. A hundred years later, it was well over 25,000 and growing fast. After the wars between Britain and Holland at the end of the eighteenth and the beginning of the nineteenth century, the Cape passed to British rule. Dutch was still the official language, and at first, the Boers were quite pleased with the change; they no longer had to live under the commercial restrictions of the Dutch East India Company. But some years later, when the British passed laws for the protection of African slaves, the Boers began to grumble.

Then in 1834, the British outlawed slavery completely. Further, they gave support to the Bantu tribesmen, who had been the main source of slaves. These two actions, which intensified the Boers' desire to leave the Cape area, were the causes of the Great Trek that began in 1835.

The object of this movement was to penetrate the unknown region beyond the Orange River, thus escaping beyond British control. The region, which would become known as the Natal, was not a complete mystery. In 1832, the Dutch Boer leaders had sent an Englishman named Dr. Andrew Smith to investigate it for a possible settlement. Smith's report had been enthusiastic. So two years later, twenty men, one woman, and a retinue of servants traveled in fourteen wagons over the same route blazed by Smith.

It was slow-going because the terrain was rocky and the rivers were swollen by the rainy season. In about six months, the Dutch party covered 400 miles, arriving in February 1825 at the sweltering hot bay of Port Natal. There, they were welcomed by a few British hunters and ivory traders - as well as the Reverend Francis Gardiner, a former Royal Navy commander, who had decided to start a mission station in Africa. Though exhausted, and relieved to be able to rest and resupply, the Boers must have also been somewhat disconcerted to find here the same people they had traveled so far to escape. But they turned back to the Cape in June, and when they arrived, gave the report that a new homeland awaited – thus setting in motion the Great Trek.

By 1837, about 2,000 persons had crossed the Orange River and settled in a number of camps on the other side.

The trekkers beyond the Orange River elected a governor, Piet Retief, who was a descendant of one of the old settler families and a man of education and talent. Retief saw that although the Boers had found freedom on the high, open plains of the interior, they now faced the possibility of being cut off from the civilized world. He determined to lead as many of his independent-minded people as would follow him across the Drakensberg Mountains into the coastal area of Natal, even though some British traders had already settled there. In February 1837, Retief published a manifesto in the *Grahamstown Journal* – a newspaper of the eastern Cape province, where many Dutch Boers still resided. It stated, in part:

> We despair of saving the colony from those evils which threaten it by the turbulent and dishonest conduct of vagrants, who are allowed to infest the country in every part; nor do we see any prospect of peace or happiness for our children in any country thus distracted by internal commotions. . . .

> We solemnly declare that we will quit this colony with a desire to lead a more quiet life than we have heretofore done. We will not molest any people, nor deprive them of the smallest property; but, if attacked, we shall consider ourselves fully justified in defending our persons and effects, to the utmost of our ability, against every enemy. . . .

> We propose, in the course of our journey, and on arriving at the country in which we shall permanently reside, to make known to the native tribes our intentions, and our desire to live in peace and friendly intercourse with them. . . .

We are now quitting the fruitful land of our birth, in which we have suffered enormous losses and continual vexation, and are entering a wild and dangerous territory; but we go with a firm reliance on an all-seeing, just, and merciful Being, whom it will be our endeavour to fear and humbly to obey.

Because of this, Retief was elected leader of "The Free Province of New Holland in South East Africa," a short-lived coalition that set out east to find a new homeland.

It took Retief's group two months to drag wagons over the mountains and down again. Often they had to dismantle the heavy carts and carry them piece by piece through crevasses and along boulder-strewn trails. On the way, also, there was constant danger from wild animals - not so much to the people themselves as to their livestock, which was their livelihood. Only by becoming machines themselves, forcing one another beyond the bounds of normal human endurance, could they survive the journey and prepare to meet the dangers which faced them on the other side of the mountains.

Only a few decades before the British traders and the Boer trekkers had arrived, the Zulus had become masters of Natal. Conquering their neighboring tribes by superior numbers and by well-organized ruthlessness, the Zulus had established themselves as undisputed overlords of the region. But their talent for murder and treachery was also their undoing: The chief who had led them on to so many victories was stabbed by his own half-brother. That bloody prince then became the Zulus' new ruler; his name was Dingaan.

At first, Dingaan was confident enough of his own mastery to greet the newcomers in a friendly manner - the British, who had arrived by sea, and the first scouts of the Boers, who were coming over the mountains. But as the Boers' numbers increased, so did Chief Dingaan's doubts.

Retief, for his part, was convinced that this was the land for his people. Its fertile valleys were ideal for both farming and grazing. He went to Dingaan and officially requested the grant of a large section. Dingaan's reply was somewhat reserved - he made the condition that the Boers get back for him some cattle that had been stolen by another tribe - but he agreed to give the land.

When word of the friendly agreement spread into the interior, more and more wagonloads of Boer families began to cross the mountains. And Dingaan's doubts turned to fear.

On February 6, 1838, he invited Retief and about forty of his men to a celebration. As soon as everyone was within the royal enclosure, the chief rose up and shouted, "Kill the wizards!" All of the white men were murdered. Retief, forced to witness the deaths of his comrades, was killed last. Their bodies were left on a hillside – called Kwa Matiwane, after a chief who had been killed there - to be eaten by vultures and scavengers. According to one story later told by the Zulus, Retief's heart and liver were buried on the road to Natal in a ceremony intended to ensure that no white men would again come that way to the king's "Great Place."

Then, the Zulus spread out to attack the newly founded settlements.

For some months, it looked as though the Zulus would triumph over the Boers as they had over the native tribes. But gradually, reinforcements arrived; the newcomers to Natal began to rally. Even so, the Boers were vastly outnumbered when, in December 1838, they launched an attack against a force of more than 12,000 Zulus.

Of the less than 700 Boers in the Battle of Blood River, 200 were servants. They were led by a farmer named Andries Pretorius – forty years old, and a descendant of the earliest line of Dutch settlers in the Cape Colony. They were armed with muskets and two cannons.

Pretorius turned out to be exceptionally skilled in strategy. He knew that his best chance at victory was to lure the Zulus out of their villages to a battleground where his men had a defensive advantage. He started by sitting down with some friendly Zulu chiefs and suggesting that the Boers were planning to build a church in Dingaan's territory - if they could reach it alive. The Zulus, he knew, saw the church as a symbol for establishing a settled state – and a way to diminish the power of Dingaan. Then, Pretorius chose a place next to a hippopotamus pool in the Ncome River and waited.

The Boers' position on the river prevented an attack from the rear; the front, meanwhile, was wide open – providing no cover for an attacking force. They gathered the wagons to make a laager (protective enclosure) and built movable wooden barriers to close the gaps between them.

Because of a Zulu superstition about the lamps that the Boers hung around the settlements, there was no danger of a night attack. The outnumbered Boers were also helped by the Zulus use of short stabbing spears instead of the longer throwing spears. At dawn on a clear December day in 1838, the first wave of Zulu warriors to charge was mown down by the Boers' muskets and cannon fire. A scribe named Jan Gerritze Bantjes recorded the battle:

> Sunday, December 16 was like being newly born for us – the sky was clear, the weather fine and bright. We hardly saw the twilight of the break of day or the guards, who were still at their posts and could just make out the distant Zulus approaching. All the patrols were called back into the laager

by firing alarm signals from the cannons. The enemy came forward at full speed and suddenly they had encircled the area around the laager. As it got lighter, so we could see them approaching over their predecessors who had already been shot back. Their rapid approach (though terrifying to witness due to their great numbers) was an impressive sight. . . . I could not count them but I was told that a captive Zulu gave the number at thirty-six regiments, each regiment calculated to be 'nine hundred to a thousand men' strong.

The battle now began and the cannons unleashed from each gate, such that the battle was fierce and noisy, even the discharging of small arms fire from our marksmen on all sides was like thunder. After more than two hours of fierce battle, the Commander in Chief gave orders that the gates be opened and mounted men sent to fight the enemy in fast attacks, as the enemy near constantly stormed the laager time and again, and he feared the ammunition would soon run out.

After three hours of fighting, about 3,000 Zulus had been killed. Only three of the Boers had been wounded, including Pretorius, on his hand. The Zulus fled in defeat, crossing a river that had turned red with blood – thereafter known as Blood River.

Chief Dingaan himself finally perished when, in 1840, he was deposed by his brother with the help of the Boers.

Though Natal was subsequently taken over by the British, the Boers had achieved their purpose of finding and developing a seacoast territory. And in the interior, they held such vast regions - the Boer Republics, as they came to be called - that there was no longer any need for expansion; the Great Trek had ended.

Yet beyond the Boer Republics stretched the whole continent of Africa, with towering mountains and undiscovered lakes large enough to be called inland seas. Trekking, the peculiar form of pioneer exploration that had been sufficient to build the new nation of South Africa, did not have the force to carry north into the central and eastern regions of the continent. That force would only be supplied by individual curiosity - curiosity about the longest river in Africa and in the world.

6

THE VICTORIAN RIVALS

In midsummer 1768, the Scottish explorer James Bruce arrived in Cairo and gazed out at the serene waters of the river that moved along the city's western border. The river was the Nile, and it was because of the river that Bruce had come to Africa. He intended to trace the Nile to its source or at least to one of its sources. He would not be the last explorer to have this mission, and he was certainly not the first.

For 2,000 years, the north-flowing Nile had been a mystery. The ancient Egyptians had sailed and poled up the river southward from its mouth at the Mediterranean to the present city of Khartoum, where two rivers, the Blue Nile and the White Nile, come together to form the mainstream. From there on, boatmen found the river unnavigable because of the great waterfalls - or cataracts - that could easily crush the sturdiest wooden vessels. And exploration on foot was made impossible by a vast swamp called the Sudd.

James Bruce's goal was to find the source of the Blue Nile, which he considered the more important of the Nile's two branches.

Bruce had come to Africa by a roundabout route. In Scotland, he had studied to be a lawyer, but after marrying the daughter of a wine importer, he went into that business instead. The wine trade had taken him to Portugal and Spain before, when Bruce was twenty-eight, his father died and left him a large estate. In London at the outbreak of Britain's war with Spain in 1762, he submitted to the British government a plan to attack the Spanish port of Ferrol. Though his plan was not adopted, it earned him the post of British consul at Algiers, where Bruce became fascinated with the study of ancient ruins. Over the next several years, that study took him to Tripoli, Benghazi, Crete, through Syria, and finally to Alexandria, where he began his endeavor to seek the source of the Nile.

He and his party set out from Cairo and got as far upriver as Aswan, where they encountered a tribal war and were forced to make a sudden detour. They headed overland to the Red Sea and sailed south to the port of Massawa. When they turned inland again, they took a southwesterly route toward Gondar.

Bruce, unlike the many men who preceded him, had a fairly accurate idea of where he was going. The source of the Blue Nile had been known centuries before; it was actually discovered in the Middle Ages by Arab traders forging into Ethiopia to look for ivory, gold, and slaves. And then in the seventeenth century, a band of Portuguese missionaries saw the river's headwaters while they were exploring the mountains of Ethiopia. They observed that a trickle of water rose in the Gojjam highlands, flowed into Lake Tana, and then became the Blue Nile. But the reports these men brought back to Europe were either ignored or forgotten. By the eighteenth century, the source of the river was still considered a geographic mystery.

For Bruce, the problem was not so much discovery as rediscovery. He hoped to settle the issue and go on record as the man who had established the exact location of the Blue Nile's headwaters.

Bruce finally reached Gondar in February 1770, and then he traveled a few miles farther south until he found Lake Tana. Part of his work had been completed; he had only to follow the river and map its course. When at last he saw the Blue Nile flow into the White Nile, he considered his mission in Africa fulfilled. His published journals from the expedition showed a flair for the dramatic: "The situation of the country was barely known, no more: placed under the most inclement of skies, in part surrounded by impenetrable forest, where from the beginning the beasts had established a sovereignty uninterrupted by man, in part by vast deserts of moving sands where nothing was to be found that had the breadth of life; these terrible barriers enclosed men more bloody and ferocious than the beasts themselves, and more fatal to travelers than the sands that encompassed them; and thus shut up, they had been long growing every day more barbarous and defied, by rendering it dangerous, the curiosity of travelers of every nation."

Bruce's account of his journey and his ultimate discovery was challenged by many of his fellow explorers in Europe. And a skeptical public found his elaborate and often overblown description of native life and scenic wonders impossible to believe. His achievement was not recognized for many years, but after his return from Africa, the interest in solving the riddle of the Nile continued to grow.

Since ancient times, men had been fascinated by the Nile. It did not behave like an ordinary river that flooded in the rainy season and dried up in a drought. Every year, in the heat of the sweltering Egyptian summer, it rose mightily over its banks and spread across the thirsty Nile Valley. Farmers depended on it, and, indeed, they worshiped it.

The river was the lifeblood of people who lived in the arid region around it. No wonder it was for so long a subject of curiosity and puzzlement.

Writing in the second century, the geographer Ptolemy, who lived in Alexandria, asserted that the Nile flowed from two lakes fed by melting snows in a region he called the "Mountains of the Moon." No one had seen Ptolemy's mountains. But no matter how hypothetical his maps may have been, they influenced explorers in Africa for hundreds of years.

Early in the eighteenth century, men began to search for the river's source by an overland route instead of defying the rapids that obstructed passage south of Egypt. Not much progress was made, however, until the mid-nineteenth-century when a pair of German missionaries arrived in Africa.

Johann Ludwig Krapf and Johannes Rebmann came to the Dark Continent to preach their faith. Both were born into farming families. Early in his schooling, Krapf developed a gift for languages – studying Latin, Greek, French, and Italian. Rebmann, meanwhile, aspired from childhood to be a "preacher and canvasser of the gospel."

But in Africa, they quickly caught the fever of exploration. Together, the two men probed the interior, mapping as they went. And the farther they went, the more intrigued they became by tales told by the natives - descriptions of giant mountains and of rich deposits of silver and gold.

They learned from a black chieftain of a "Country of the Moon" which lay, it was said, near some magnificent inland lakes. Might not this region be the "Mountains of the Moon" about which Ptolemy had written? Krapf and Rebmann hoped to find out. They continued their exploration into the tropical heart of East Africa, and before they turned back discovered two towering mountains covered with snow. Somewhere in that mountain area, they felt certain, lay the source of the White Nile.

But no one in Europe would listen to them. Their report received ridicule instead of praise, for who could believe that snow-capped mountains existed on the equator? It was proved later that the two Germans had discovered Mount Kilimanjaro and Mount Kenya, which are not near the source of the White Nile. The "Mountains of the Moon" (now called the Ruwenzori), which they believed they had seen, are farther west, between Uganda and the Congo. It was in this region that the headwaters of the White Nile were eventually found.

Despite the fact that Krapf and Rebmann's report of their achievements was rejected by the so-called experts of their day, England was encouraged to send an expedition to the part of East Africa that the German missionaries had mapped. England's interest in this region had increased substantially since the

1830s when the coastal areas of present-day Kenya and Tanganyika came under her influence. And the Royal Geographical Society was now convinced that the headwaters of the White Nile might be reached by land. The society favored a route originating in the east, and for a very good reason. Since the Niger had proved to have no connection with the Nile, it seemed likely that the source of the White Nile was in the east, not the west.

In 1856, the Royal Geographical Society chose two men, Richard Francis Burton and John Hanning Speke, to journey overland through East Africa to look for the headwaters of the great river. With this undertaking, a new phase of exploration began; the great age of African discovery was approaching its climax.

Although they shared a common interest in exploration in general and Africa in particular, Burton and Speke were wholly different men.

Burton was well-educated and well-traveled; by one count, he spoke twenty-nine European, Asian, and African languages. At the urging of some of his college classmates, he had enlisted in the British Army's East India Company, hoping to fight in the first Afghan war, but it was over by the time he reached India. As a soldier, he said, he was "fit for nothing but to be shot at for six pence a day."

Speke, on the other hand, was a military man. Commissioned as an officer in the British Indian Army at age seventeen, he served honorably under Sir Colin Campbell during the First Anglo-Sikh War. During military leave, he explored the Himalayan Mountains and Mount Everest, and once crossed into Tibet.

Burton, who was thirty-six at the time of the expedition, made good use of his gift for languages. In order to learn more about the Indians, he frequently wore Eastern clothes and often dyed his face and hands so he could mingle freely and unnoticed.

Burton had a flair for flamboyance that Speke did not share. Speke was six years younger than Burton, and by contrast was quiet and conventional. He lived up to the ideal of what a young man of the Victorian Age should be. He rarely drank, never smoked, and seemed to be without humor, at least on the surface. He was devoted to the study of natural history, and his favorite forms of relaxation were hunting and shooting.

Before he was yet twenty-one years old, Speke had been struck by an urge to visit Africa. His purpose at that time had merely been to collect rare birds and animals for the natural history museum he was building in his father's home in Somerset, England. When leave was granted him, after ten years' military service, he asked permission to go to Africa and was advised to join an expedition headed by Richard Burton.

So the two men had explored in Africa for the first time in 1854. They knew the country, and they had learned to get along with each other. Thus, when Burton was selected to lead another expedition with the specific purpose of finding the source of the White Nile, it was logical for him to ask Speke to accompany him. In December 1856, the two men arrived in Zanzibar, where their expedition to the interior was to begin.

Zanzibar is a tiny island lying off the coast of modern Tanganyika. At the time of Burton and Speke's arrival, the capital city had a population of 100,000 and was the main depot for the slave and ivory trade to the East. Although commerce in slaves had been officially banned by the British, it was carried on illegally and at great profit. Men and women waiting to be shipped out of the country wandered through the narrow streets, naked, bewildered, often hungry and sick. As a result, cholera, smallpox, and malaria raged through the town, and dead slaves were cast away on the beaches to rot.

Zanzibar was deplorable, but it could also be beautiful. The town provided splendid comforts to those who could afford them. At times, it seemed the model of a lazy tropical isle.

When he reached Zanzibar, Burton immediately began arranging for a caravan to the interior. His expedition, when finally organized, was composed of more than 100 carriers, servants, and guards. In addition, he enlisted about twenty soldiers from the sultan of Zanzibar and hired two personal servants who would act as cooks.

Among the supplies brought along on the expedition were some of the latest European weapons and scientific instruments plus tents, camp beds, tables, chairs, air pillows, and a small library. There were also carpenters' and blacksmiths' tools and a portable boat. For himself and his young associate, Burton took along a dozen bottles of brandy, a box of cigars, thirty pounds of tea, and a medicine chest that contained a good supply of quinine. This medicine had been used for some time to fight malaria, but unfortunately, Burton did not have much faith in it.

The men moved their supplies and the carriers they had been able to hire in Zanzibar to the mainland. Here at the village of Bagamoyo, they discovered that only thirty-six more porters were available. It became necessary to buy a number of donkeys - at prices much higher than the cost of buying men - and to leave much of the heavier baggage behind, including the portable boat. Finally, the caravan set out on June 25, 1857.

The coastal plain of East Africa can be hot and

unpleasant, but about 100 miles inland, the terrain rises to a wind-swept plateau. This tableland, which averages about 3,000 feet in height, extends across East and Central Africa to the western Congo. Thus, the part of the continent that follows the equator is less a land of steaming jungles than one of rolling hills and high plateaus. Once they had reached the plateau country, Burton and Speke realized that the presence of tall mountains, as reported by Krapf and Rebmann, was certainly not improbable.

The expedition was soon able to recruit more carriers, and finally, it numbered 132 persons. They were now heading toward Kazeh, an Arab trading post situated two-thirds of the way between the Indian Ocean and Lake Tanganyika. This town, today called Tabora, is the modern junction of railroad lines from the lake country of the north and west. The caravan arrived there in November 1857, after a five-month journey. The men had averaged about 100 miles a month; their trip so far had been quite comfortable under the circumstances.

Burton was overjoyed to see the Arabs in Kazeh. Because he spoke Arabic fluently, he felt that he was again among friends. Moreover, he had developed an intense dislike of the blacks - a feeling that Speke never shared or condoned. This difference in attitude caused considerable friction between the two men. They were growing cooler to each other, and from this point on, Burton's journal rarely mentioned Speke except to ridicule him.

The fact is that they had not been the best of friends when the expedition began. Their relationship had been scarred by the disastrous ending of their first African adventure when they were attacked by some fierce Somali tribesmen. During the encounter, Speke ran back to the protection of his tent. He did this, he said later, so he could get a clearer view of his attackers, but Burton misunderstood his movements. Burton called out, "Don't step back or they will think we are retiring!"

Speke could only assume that this was meant as a comment on his courage. He was wounded in this encounter and then captured and tortured. But long after the wounds had healed and the pain had been forgotten, Burton's words continued to rankle. This incident in itself did not bring about a breach between the two men, but the hatred they later felt for each other could probably be traced back to it.

Early in December 1857, Burton and Speke headed west from Kazeh, and the following February discovered Lake Tanganyika. On the shores of the lake was an Arab trading post called Ujiji, which had been established barely a dozen years before.

Burton and Speke's discovery of Lake Tanganyika was a major event. Whatever else happened, their expedition could now be considered a success, but both men were seriously ill. Burton had suffered from continual bouts with malaria since leaving Kazeh, and now he was afflicted with a painful abscess that had developed in his jaw. Speke had become nearly blind from the sudden worsening of an eye disease that had troubled him since his childhood. Thus, he described the expedition's first view of the lake rather dryly: "From the summit of the eastern horn, the lovely Tanganyika Lake could be seen in all its glory by everyone but myself."

When Speke's eyesight at last improved, the two men made a hurried exploration of the lake that Burton believed was the source of the White Nile. This began to seem unlikely, however, because their instruments indicated that the lake was only ten feet higher than the known level of the White Nile at Gondokoro, almost 600 miles to the north. Burton knew that the descent of any river must be steeper than that to hold to its banks, but he was not yet willing to concede defeat. He wanted to investigate further, but his illness had so weakened him that he had to return to Ujiji.

In June 1858, the caravan arrived in Kazeh. Burton was much in need of rest and eager to complete his notes on the progress of the trip. Thus, when an Arab trader described another lake - this one bigger and perhaps at a higher altitude than Tanganyika - Speke requested permission to go off and see it himself. Burton let him go, possibly with some relief, and the younger man took along one gun carrier and a small party of porters and guards.

In exactly twenty-five days, Speke reached the great lake that the natives called Ukerewe and which he christened Victoria after England's reigning queen. He was convinced, the moment he saw the lake, that it was the long-sought source of the White Nile. Later he wrote: "The caravan . . . began winding up a long but gradually inclined hill - which, as it bears no name, I shall call Somerset - until it reached its summit, when the vast expanse of the pale blue waters of the [lake] burst suddenly on my gaze. It was early morning. The distant sea line of the north horizon was defined in the calm atmosphere between the north and west points of the compass . . . I no longer felt any doubt that the lake at my feet gave birth to that interesting river, the source of which has been the subject of so much speculation, and the object of so many explorers."

Speke hurried back to Kazeh to inform the ailing Burton of his discovery. The older man was unimpressed by his assistant's assertion that he had found the source of the White Nile. As usual, Burton ridiculed him and succeeded in making Speke more adamant. They argued bitterly.

Speke was substantially right, and his chief was wrong, but Burton's contention was not motivated entirely by jealousy. As Speke had seen but a small portion of the lake's south shore, his convictions could be based only on supposition. He had merely had an "inspiration," as Burton pointedly reminded him, and that was by no means conclusive proof.

Neither man would back down, and the argument was finally abandoned. In September of that year, the two explorers loaded their caravan and began the long return trip to the coast. By this time, both men were desperately ill - Burton with malaria and Speke with pneumonia and pleurisy. They were so weak they had to be carried, and the caravan did not reach the African coast until February 1859. From there, they made their way to Aden, a settlement on the southwest coast of Arabia.

Burton remained in Aden in an attempt to recuperate while Speke immediately booked passage to England. They agreed that nothing should be published about their exploration unless they both could take credit for it. And before he embarked, Speke gave Burton his word that he would disclose nothing about the expedition until Burton himself had arrived in London.

Speke did not keep his promise. The strength of his conviction apparently got the better of him, and when he arrived in London, he went straight to the Royal Geographical Society and made the claim that he had discovered the source of the White Nile. Moreover, the society accepted his findings and later asked him to return to Africa at the head of his own expedition.

When Richard Burton at last landed in England, still weak from illness, he found himself almost completely forgotten. His report on Lake Tanganyika as the true source of the White Nile was received coolly and without much interest. Wrong or right, he was treated badly, and he never forgave his former subordinate, John Speke, as long as the young man lived.

7
FOUNTAINS OF THE NILE

The man Speke chose to accompany him on his return trip to Lake Victoria proved a perfect second-in-command. James Augustus Grant was the same age as Speke, trustworthy, and submissive as well - qualities of character that Speke himself had not displayed when he served under Burton. Grant, born in the Scottish Highlands, was the son of a minister, and a soldier in the British Indian Army from the age of twenty-one. He had an interest in botany, and during the expedition would make many valuable plant collections. Best of all, he showed absolute loyalty to his comrade.

As Grant later wrote in his book, *A Walk Across Africa,* "Not a shade of jealousy or distrust or even ill temper ever came between us." As these were precisely the feelings that had come between Burton and Speke, the virtue in this particular case must have been wholly Grant's.

The two men set out from Zanzibar with a large caravan in September 1860. It took them more than a year to reach the unknown plateau country west of Lake Tanganyika. In that high heartland of Central Africa, Speke and Grant came upon three native kingdoms that made up part of the present country of Uganda. For centuries, people who lived to the west and north of the lake had been building a civilization that was almost completely cut off from the outside world. Karagwe in the south was the weakest of their three states. Buganda and Bunyoro in the north were the strongest and were bitter rivals.

The travelers remained awhile in Karagwe, where the king treated them cordially. Then early in 1862, they headed north - all except Grant, who had a painful leg sore that made walking impossible.

In Buganda, Speke insisted on being treated as a visiting noble instead of as a trader. He was granted an audience with the king, but the explorer fumed at being made to wait in the hot sun until the king was ready to receive him. After a few minutes' pause, Speke turned on his heel and returned to camp.

The king's courtiers were dumbfounded, for no

visitor had ever behaved so imperiously. They ran after Speke and urged him to return with them to the palace, assuring him that their leader would see him right away. They even gave him permission to bring a chair to sit on during the interview. This was unprecedented, for no man but the chief was ever allowed to sit on anything but earth.

When he arrived at the royal court, Speke presented the native king with a number of gifts, including, pointedly, an iron chair, as well as several carbines and a revolver. In the book he later wrote, Speke described the king as "a good-looking, well-figured, tall young man of twenty-five" whom he found "sitting on a red blanket spread upon a square platform of royal grass encased in tiger reeds."

For an hour, the two men, native king and English explorer, sat and stared at each other without exchanging a word. Then when it was growing dark, a messenger approached the explorer to ask if he had seen the king. "Yes, for one full hour," Speke replied rather testily. When this reply was translated for the king, he rose to his feet, took his spear in hand, and silently left the enclosure. He walked on his toes in imitation, it was said, of a lion.

Speke was stunned. Had he been insulted? No, not at all, he was assured. Actually, he had been treated very courteously because the king, who was now eating dinner, had delayed having his meal until Speke arrived for the interview.

Speke continued to be treated respectfully throughout his stay, perhaps because he had established his right to royal privilege. After Speke had spent three months in Buganda, Grant arrived, his condition improved despite a lingering limp. The men made plans to leave Buganda, but the king was not eager to let them go. He enjoyed the presence of white men in his court. Besides, he was convinced that the longer they stayed, the more gifts he could get them to give him. He delayed their departure for six more weeks; finally, on July 7, 1862, he allowed them to depart.

The men headed north toward a river they believed to be the first stage of the White Nile. This river, now called the Victoria Nile, runs northwest between Lake Victoria and a body of water that was discovered two years later and named Lake Albert. Speke followed this river alone for some time, having sent Grant to open up the way to Bunyoro, the third native kingdom in the region. On July 28, Speke came to a series of rapids. They were only thirteen feet high but very broad, and from the volume of water that poured over them, Speke was certain he had seen the first outpouring of a great river.

In his book, Speke described the rapids as "a sight that attracted one to it for hours - the roar of the waters, the thousands of passenger fish leaping at the falls with all their might . . . hippopotamuses and crocodiles lying sleepily on the water . . . and cattle driven down to drink."

He named these rapids Ripon Falls, after Lord Ripon, the man who had presided over the Royal Geographical Society at the time Speke's expedition was organized. Now the explorer was certain he had reached his goal and that his work was done. He was not certain, however, that he and Grant could stay alive long enough to find their way out again to tell the news. Their supplies were dangerously low, and they were both exhausted.

Cutting across country as quickly as he could, Speke rejoined Grant, and together the two men and their caravan - now vastly reduced because of disease and desertion - marched into Bunyoro. King Kamrasi, who ruled this land, was a moody and suspicious man, and a greedy one, too. He robbed them of much of their remaining supplies before they could get away. At last, they moved northward again. Their only hope, they thought, was to meet a relief expedition that was supposed to reach them with fresh supplies and additional carriers. The explorers were a year late for the rendezvous, and they were afraid they might have been given up for lost.

But the slim hope of rescue drove them on. They tramped through jungle and scrubland and across vast stretches of grassland. And whenever they could, they floated downstream on the Nile.

All around them were hostile tribes of painted natives, fiercer and more primitive than any they had encountered before. One time these natives attacked the caravan, in Speke's words, "dancing like so many devils, with sheaves of burning grass in their hands."

On February 15, 1863, Speke and Grant stumbled into the upper Nile trading station of Gondokoro. There, to their surprise and joy, they were met by a hearty Englishman named Samuel Baker. He and his wife had come up the Nile hoping to find them.

"What joy this was I can hardly tell," wrote Speke, who had known Baker many years before. "We could not talk fast enough, so overwhelmed were we both to meet again." Soon Speke and Grant also encountered the official relief expedition that had come to rescue them, and then sailed down the Nile to Cairo. When they finally returned to London more than two-and-a-half years after they had left, they were greeted warmly by the Royal Geographical Society, which had sent them, and by a public that had waited for them anxiously.

Meanwhile, the Bakers continued their journey, taking up the task of Nile exploration themselves. To almost anyone but Samuel Baker, the thought of bringing a woman into the wilds of an uncharted country would have seemed foolhardy - particularly when the odds against survival were so great. But Baker was a most uncommon man, and his wife was a remarkable woman.

Samuel White Baker, born in London, was the son of a wealthy merchant, banker, and ship owner. He was known for his exploits as a big-game hunter in Asia, Europe, and North America. With his first wife, Henrietta, he had seven children; then, after twelve years of marriage, she died of typhoid fever. His second wife, Florence, had been orphaned and sold as a slave when she was fourteen years old. She was twenty years younger than Baker. Some accounts claim that Baker was on a hunting trip in Vidin, on the southern bank of the Danube River in Bulgaria, when he saw Florence about to be sold to the local pasha, or governor. Supposedly, he bribed some guards and took ownership of her himself. They fled to Bucharest, where they were married, and from then, were inseparable. Florence did more than tag along on his voyages. Fluent in English, Turkish, and Arabic, she charmed the natives, who called her "*Anyadwe*," or "Daughter of the Moon." She rode camels, mules, and horses; and carried pistols. So it was no surprise for her to accompany him to Africa.

Their undertaking proved every bit as hazardous as that of Burton, Speke, and Grant, and the Bakers acquitted themselves brilliantly.

They had arrived in Africa in 1861 while Speke and Grant were still plodding through Tanganyika. Since Baker and his wife were under no instructions from any scientific or religious society, they could do exactly as they pleased. They hoped to meet Speke and Grant on the way up the Nile, but they had other plans as well. After spending fourteen months exploring the tributaries that flowed from Ethiopia into the great river, they went to Khartoum in June 1862 and prepared for a journey up the White Nile.

Khartoum, at the time the Bakers went there, had been in existence only forty years. Like Zanzibar, it was a trading post for exchanging slaves and ivory. Samuel and Florence detested the place and wanted to leave it as soon as possible. Yet it took them six months to acquire three ships and 100 men to take them up the Nile to Gondokoro.

The traders in Khartoum, afraid the Bakers would try to stop the capturing of slaves, did not want them to go farther south. The town's Egyptian governor even sent an official to halt the expedition. But Baker threatened to toss him overboard and the official backed down. As it happened, Samuel Baker was not an abolitionist.

The Bakers and their flotilla left for Gondokoro in December 1862. When they arrived, they deposited all their stores with an Egyptian merchant, with instructions to give half to Speke and Grant is they happened to arrive.

These instructions proved needless. Thirteen

days after the Bakers came to Gondokoro, Speke and Grant - and the remnants of their weary caravan - pulled into town. Considering the delays endured by each party, the timing of this meeting seems incredible. The Bakers were not surprised to see the two Englishmen despite the odd coincidence, but they were disappointed that they had not shared in the discovery of the source of the White Nile. Baker even said to Speke, with characteristic candor, "Does not one leaf of the laurel remain for me?" Speke replied by assuring Baker that there was, in fact, a whole branch of laurel left to pick. As Baker later wrote: "[Speke] gave me a map of their route showing that they had been unable to complete the actual exploration of the Nile, and that a most important portion still remained to be determined . . . I now heard that the field was not only open but that additional interest was given to the exploration by the proof that the Nile flowed out of one great lake, the Victoria, but that it evidently must derive an additional supply from an unknown lake as it entered [this lake] at the northern extremity."

Immediately they decided they would have to see this "unknown lake." The Bakers had seen Speke's map and knew where they were going, but the way was not without hardship and peril. They set out in March 1863, and by the end of the year, they had to buy and train three oxen to replace their exhausted horses.

Soon Baker began to suffer from attacks of fever. He had brought along quinine, and he and his wife had used it faithfully. But as they had been away from Gondokoro for ten months, their supply was exhausted. In the beginning, Florence suffered from disease far less than her husband and generally bore up admirably under the strain of travel. She was never frightened by the thumping of war drums or the sight of savages dancing. And if she heard the stealthy tread of an intruder sneaking into camp at night, she would awaken her husband calmly. "She was not a *screamer*," he wrote of her, which summed up her character and at the same time praised it succinctly.

Near the end of January, the Bakers managed to get themselves ferried across the Victoria Nile. On February 10, 1864, they reached Bunyoro. King Kamrasi was as surly to them as he had been to Speke and Grant. And he extorted from them almost everything they possessed. The couple was nearly helpless because by now fever gripped them both. Defying illness and exhaustion, they pushed on toward the lake, which was only a few weeks' march away.

Before long, Florence grew too weak to do much walking; there were times when she had to be carried on a litter fashioned from wicker bedsteads. At one point, when a swampy river barred the way, the caravan crossed carefully on a natural bridge composed of piled-up vegetation. Here is how Baker described the crossing: "I led the way, and begged Mrs. Baker to follow me on foot as quickly as possible, precisely in my tracks. The river was about eighty yards wide, and I had scarcely completed a fourth of the distance and looked back to see if my wife followed close to me when I was horrified to see her standing in one spot and sinking gradually through the weeds while her face was distorted and perfectly purple."

The explorer rushed back and managed to rescue her. "I dragged her," he wrote, "like a corpse through the yielding vegetation, and up to our waists we scrambled across to the other side, just keeping her head above water." When they reached the opposite bank, Baker realized that his wife was suffering from sunstroke.

As there was no food here, the caravan pressed on two more days, and porters carried the unconscious woman. Baker kept watch over her for two days - until on the third morning, she awoke delirious. It was raining now as Baker and his carriers continued their march, searching desperately for food. As Baker later recalled: "For seven days I had not slept, and although as weak as a reed, I had marched by the side of her litter. Nature could resist no longer. We reached a village one evening; she had been in violent convulsions successively - it was all but over. I laid her down on her litter within a hut, covered her with a Scotch plaid, and I fell upon my mat insensible, worn out with sorrow and fatigue. My men put a new handle to the pickaxe that evening and sought for a dry spot to dig her grave."

But Florence Baker was not to be counted out yet. When her husband awoke after his own collapse, he found her calm and well again; after two days' convalescence, she was ready to resume the journey.

At daybreak on March 14, 1864, the caravan reached the summit of a low hill. And there, as Baker reported, "The glory of our prize burst suddenly before me! There, like a sea of quicksilver, lay . . . the grand expanse of water - a boundless sea-horizon on the south and southwest, glittering in the noonday sun . . ." There was a zigzag path down to the water, but this was so steep that the oxen they were riding could not negotiate it. But the Bakers could and did. Supported by a stick of stout bamboo and "strengthened by success," they tottered down the cliff and walked through sandy meadows to the water's edge.

"The waves were rolling upon a white pebbly beach," Baker recalled. "I rushed into the lake, and thirsty with heat and fatigue, with a heart full of gratitude, I drank deeply from the sources of the Nile." And then, as "an imperishable memorial of one loved and mourned by our gracious queen . . . I called this great lake the Albert . . . The Victoria and Albert lakes are the two sources of the Nile."

The Bakers had reached their objective and enjoyed their moment of triumph. Now they had to get back. They obtained crude canoes from some native fishermen and proceeded north along the shores of Lake Albert. They finally reached the point where the Victoria Nile enters the lake. Sailing upstream, they came upon a magnificent waterfall. Baker named it Murchison Falls after Sir Roderick Murchison, who had become president of the Royal Geographical Society.

The return trip overland proved as perilous as the first leg of the journey. But who could doubt that the Bakers would get through? When they reached England at last, Samuel Baker was knighted, and Florence Baker, now Lady Baker, very promptly became the rage of London society. Loyally, and in all sincerity, Baker gave credit to "the devoted companion of my pilgrimage, to whom I owed success and life - my wife."

Before they arrived in England, however, the Bakers were shocked and aggrieved to learn of the death of the man who had made their success possible, John Hanning Speke. They also learned that though Speke and Grant had been widely acclaimed upon returning to England, there was still some doubt as to the measure of the men's achievement. After all, it was said, Speke had not followed the entire course of the river that flowed out of Lake Victoria.

Therefore, it was not inconceivable that the Nile might have yet another source. Richard Burton was one of the strongest proponents of this argument, and soon, a full-blown controversy raged.

At last it was decided that Burton and Speke should confront each other at a public meeting. The younger man dreaded the encounter, probably because he knew how persuasive Burton could be. At any rate, the encounter was never held. While Burton was on the platform and the audience had been kept waiting twenty-five minutes, word came that Speke had been killed in a hunting accident. There was some polite Victorian speculation at the time that Speke's death had really been suicide, and for a while, it seemed that Burton had won his point - and had been avenged.

This victory, however sweet, was not long-lasting. The report that the Bakers brought back to England the following year tended to substantiate Speke's findings. But still there were many people who doubted his theories, and to a certain extent, their doubts may have been justified. It had been proved that the Victoria Nile ran from Lake Victoria to Lake Albert. It had also been shown that a river issued toward the north from Lake Albert and that this river was probably the White Nile.

But what about Lake Albert itself? Baker had not explored the entire circumference of the lake; thus, if there should prove to be a river entering the lake at its southern end, that river might have to be considered the true source of the Nile. This was by no means an outlandish idea. Lake Edward lies just south of Lake Albert, and south of that is Lake Kivu, which is in turn connected to Lake Tanganyika by the Ruzizi River. If all these lakes had actually been joined, then Lake Tanganyika would be the true source of the Nile - just as Burton had insisted.

Since the question was still unsettled, the Royal Geographical Society decided to send out one other man to try and solve the mystery. This man, who was destined to become the greatest explorer of his time, was David Livingstone.

8
DR. LIVINGSTONE

David Livingstone was born at Blantyre, Scotland, on March 23, 1813. His father was a Sunday school teacher, who passed out Christian tracts door-to-door, influencing his son's later missionary zeal. David went to work in a cotton mill when he was ten so that he could earn money to buy his own books, which he managed to read while working at his spinning machine. Later, he worked summers at the mill and studied medicine and theology in the winter at nearby Glasgow. Then, in 1840, he sailed for Cape Town to become a medical missionary in Africa.

Unlike such men as Samuel Baker and Richard Burton, Livingstone had a high regard for the African natives. He was shocked by what he saw of the African slave trade that still flourished in the 1840s even though it had been officially outlawed.

Slave merchants had been among the very first explorers in Africa. Their arrival in a new territory resembled an invasion because they raided villages and burned homes in cruel assaults. Their objective was to capture the hardiest specimens and drag them aboard the jam-packed slave ships. The slave trade expanded as the demand for slaves increased in Mediterranean countries and in the East. And because so many Africans themselves contributed to the flow of slave traffic, any attempt to abolish slavery seemed futile. Native chieftains had turned into small-time tycoons, trading their tribesmen for trinkets, and the work of the slavers was becoming not only less difficult but more profitable.

Antislavery interests tried to encourage other forms of trade among the natives as a way to end slavery. They were certain that slavery could not continue if the African continent were opened up fully to commerce and colonization. This was called the positive policy for achieving abolition, and young David Livingstone was soon one of its greatest exponents.

His first station in Africa was at Kuruman, about 120 miles northwest of Kimberley on the southern edge of the Kalahari Desert. There he set about visiting neighboring settlements and learning the native Bechuana language. Dr. Robert Moffat was chief of the mission station, and in 1844, Livingstone married Moffat's oldest daughter, Mary. During the next few years, Livingstone and his wife built several more mission stations, but by this time, the young doctor was becoming more and more eager to strike deeper into the interior. He had heard that a "land of waters and forests" existed beyond Lake Ngami at the far side of the Kalahari Desert, and his curiosity had been aroused.

In 1849, two wealthy game hunters, William C. Oswell and Mungo Murray, came to Africa. They invited Livingstone to act as interpreter and accompany their hunting party on an expedition north across the desert. Two months later, they reached Lake Ngami in the western part of Bechuanaland what is now Botswana. They were probably the first white men to see that region. Compared to what Livingstone later accomplished, however, this was no great feat of exploration, but it did excite considerable interest back in England. In 1851, the doctor traveled north again with Oswell and at Sesheke discovered the rushing waters of the upper Zambezi River.

Peering across the river that wound through woodland and meadow, Livingstone could not help wondering where it went. Did it connect with the Congo? Did it flow into one of the rivers at the source of the Nile? Livingstone was determined to find out, but floods and malaria kept him from following the river then.

Yet he remained convinced of the commercial importance of his discovery of the Zambezi. As he wrote in a letter to his parents, the slave trade had only recently come to the region around Sesheke, which was occupied by a people known as the Makololo. He had extracted a promise from the Makololo not to barter in slaves, but Livingstone believed that "the only effectual means of putting a stop to the trade would be to supply the market with English goods in exchange for the products of their country." And what better avenue for this trade than the Zambezi itself?

"I feel assured," wrote Livingstone, "that if Christian merchants would establish a legitimate commerce on the Zambezi they would drive slave dealers out of the market and would certainly be no losers in the end." Initially, at least, his desire to explore the Zambezi was prompted by a passionate belief that if he succeeded in marking out trade routes in southern Africa, the institution of slavery would topple.

In April 1852, he returned to Cape Town with his wife and children, whom he then sent back to England. Next, he set about collecting supplies for another expedition to the north. The Boers (Dutch settlers) at the Cape were not friendly. They wanted no interference with slavery, so they spread reports that Livingstone had sold arms to the natives and had tried to incite a rebellion. Boers attacked Livingstone's last mission station at Kolobeng and destroyed all his belongings.

By the following year, Livingstone had penetrated deep into the country east of Lake Ngami. At last, in May 1853, he came to Linyanti, the Makololo capital, where he was welcomed by the chief of the tribe. Livingstone's plan was to sail upstream on the Zambezi and eventually strike out westward across the continent to the port city of Loanda (now Luanda) on the west coast of Portuguese Angola.

A party of Makololo agreed to accompany him, and they made the journey by boat and by land. It was Livingstone's custom to travel light, for his needs were few. At first, the party advanced without undue hardships. But by early 1854, the food supply was short, and when the rainy season came, the entire party found itself sloshing uncomfortably across meadows that were ankle deep in water. Malaria and dysentery were rampant, and at one point, the men, weary of the miserable journey, threatened to mutiny. Recalling the grim occasion, Livingstone wrote, "Knowing that our lives depended on vigorously upholding authority, I seized a double-barreled pistol and darted out looking, I suppose, so savage as to put them to flight." He never had trouble with his men again.

By April 1854, the expedition had arrived at Cassange, which was a relatively large Portuguese trading station. The first European Livingstone met there asked to see his passport and then explained that the explorer would have to be taken to the authorities. Livingstone was delighted to go, for as he explained, he was "very much in the position of people who commit a minor offense if only to obtain board and lodging in prison." However, the commandant of the station fed him without jailing him, gave him a change of clothing, and according to Livingstone, "treated me as though I were his own brother."

Proceeding west and slightly north from Cassange and crossing densely wooded country, Livingstone approached the coast on May 15. Then, on May 31, he reached Loanda. As he had not fared well under attacks of malaria, he was urged by the English naval officers he met to return at once to England. He declined, however, noting: "My task is only half completed; I want to go back to Linyanti and try from there to press on to the east coast. Perhaps it is there that the better way is to be found for trade contacts with the interior."

For a long time, Livingstone had been aware that the upper course of the Zambezi was for the most part unnavigable and frequently impassable. But he felt fairly certain that eastward from the Makololo territory, where he had first seen the river, the Zambezi might be a useful avenue of trade extending to the Indian Ocean. Though he had accomplished a tremendous feat by reaching Loanda overland, he could not end his expedition there. He had promised his Makololo porters that he would bring them back home again even though doing so would mean traveling another 2,000 miles, mostly on foot. There was never any question in Livingstone's mind that he would keep that promise, and he did.

It took them a whole year to get back to Linyanti, which was roughly 100 miles west of the present city of Livingstone in Northern Rhodesia. No journey quite like it had ever been attempted.

In November 1855, after several months' rest in Linyanti, Livingstone headed east to complete his crossing of the continent. He reached the coast at Quelimane in Mozambique six months later. His health was broken when he finally returned to England, but he was acclaimed a hero. Probably no man of his time had so fired the public imagination. He was persuaded to write an account of his experiences, and when this was published in 1857, under the title *Missionary Travels*, it was an immediate success.

Dr. Livingstone returned to the Zambezi in 1859 at the head of an expedition that included his younger brother Charles and Dr. John Kirk, who later became acting British consul at

Zanzibar. Livingstone had been entrusted with the responsibility of gathering more information about the natives, exploring the possibilities for British trade in central and eastern Africa, and continuing to combat slavery.

He and his party had a steamship called the *Ma-Robert* which they wanted to take up the Zambezi River from the African east coast. But the stiff current was too much for the vessel, and she was soon forced to turn back. Now it was obvious to Livingstone that the Zambezi was wholly useless as an avenue of trade. He requested a new steamship from England, and when it arrived, he sailed up the Shire River, which connects with the lower Zambezi. Then, through a deep gorge in the mountains, he sighted Lake Nyasa. Two years later, he returned to explore his discovery.

At the beginning of 1862, he sailed east to the mouth of the Zambezi to meet his wife, who had come back from England. But by the time he reached the coast, Mary Livingstone had caught a tropical fever, and she soon died.

Three years later, Livingstone accepted the invitation of the Royal Geographical Society to return to Central Africa - this time to clarify, once and for all, the mysteries shrouding its water courses. At fifty-three, he may have seemed too old for the strenuous life of an African explorer. However, his was a hardy nature, and after the loss of his wife, he had little reason to remain in England.

Much exploration had already taken place at this time in the area on either side of the chain of lakes extending from Lake Albert in the north to Lake Nyasa in the south. Baker had probed into this region from the north; Burton, Speke, and Grant had made inroads from the east; and Livingstone himself had made discoveries in the south. But a large portion of the territory was still unexplored, and Livingstone hoped now to be the man to explore it.

He had become convinced that the true source of the White Nile was actually a river that arose in Lake Mweru, southwest of Lake Tanganyika. And he knew that this river flowed into a much larger stream to the north called the Lualaba. But he knew nothing about the Lualaba except that it, too, flowed north. Was it the Nile or some unknown river? Could it be the Congo? (Its source had not yet been found.) That, too, was a possibility.

Heavy rainfall punished the countryside as Livingstone and his party cut their way toward the southern end of Lake Tanganyika. His recurring bouts with illness loosened his teeth and also slowed his advance. Soon his supplies were nearly spent, and he was forced to head for Ujiji on the eastern shore of the lake, where goods from the coast were supposedly waiting for him. In February 1869, he reached the lake, almost toothless and nearly dead from exhaustion. He was, he wrote, "a ruckle of bones."

At Ujiji, he found that his supplies had been looted. He remained there, however, in a native hut, trying to restore what he could of his health. After six months, he was back on his feet. He crossed Lake Tanganyika and headed west toward the Lualaba, which he reached in March 1871, at the town of Nyangwe.

Livingstone was hopeful, if not absolutely certain, that the Lualaba was really the upper White Nile. He was wrong, but he never knew it. The Lualaba is actually the upper Congo, the last of Africa's four great waterways to be explored to its source.

The weary explorer stood on the bank of the majestic river as it flowed north toward cataracts that were later named Stanley Falls. What lay beyond the mountains, beyond the thick, dark forests through which the river was known to pass? Livingstone knew he would have to attempt to find out. He tried to acquire boats for a downriver expedition, but the Arabs, suspicious that he might eventually bring other Englishmen to tap their copper mines, denied him assistance. Nor were the blacks very helpful, so frightened were they of the arrogant slave merchants. After several fruitless weeks, Livingstone's lack of supplies forced him to abandon his plans. He returned, sick and starving, to Ujiji.

Seven hundred miles lay between him and the coast, and he was too weak to attempt the journey. He was not lost, merely unable to continue. He had to depend on the generosity of the Arabs to stay alive; he was practically reduced to begging. Then one day, less than a month after he had arrived, a splendidly equipped caravan rumbled into the lakeside village, flying, of all things, an American flag.

It was November 10, 1871. There was excitement in the village that day because the caravan was turned out so impressively. Roused by one of his servants, the old doctor went out to greet the newcomers. He stood among a group of Arabs observing the enormous train of supplies being unloaded. Suddenly a white man approached him - a short man, and stocky, with a look of supreme exultation on his face.

"Dr. Livingstone, I presume?" the white man asked.

"Yes," replied the missionary, lifting his cap slightly.

"I thank God, Doctor, I have been permitted to see you," said the white man, who identified himself as Henry Morton Stanley.

And Livingstone replied, "I feel thankful that I am here to welcome you."

This then became the most-celebrated encounter in the history of African exploration. The two men were more than a generation apart, and perhaps a world apart in their thinking. Only a trick of fate had brought them together here in the heart of the African wilderness. Surely no two men could have been so different, not even Burton and Speke.

The man who called himself Henry M. Stanley was born in Wales in 1841, the year that Livingstone first went to Africa. He received what little education he had in a workhouse, where he and the other able-bodied poor exchanged their labors for food and lodging. When he was sixteen, he took a job as cabin boy on a ship and went to America. There he was befriended by a rich New Orleans merchant who became his protector.

The boy, whose real name was John Rowlands, became deeply attached to the merchant - so much so that when the older man died, the boy took his name: Henry Morton Stanley.

During the next decade, Stanley's life in America was a turbulent one. He fought with both the Union and Confederate armies in the Civil War and served for a while in the U.S. Navy. He became a reporter, first in Missouri and then in New York City. As a foreign correspondent for the *New York Herald*, he was soon recognized as a leading journalist.

In 1869, his editor, James Gordon Bennett Jr., sent him to Africa to cover the opening of the Suez Canal. After this, he traveled east as far as India, filing stories as he went, and then returned to Africa to search for David Livingstone. The aging missionary had been heard from only twice in the four years since he had left England, and Bennett was certain that Livingstone's rescue would provide the basis for a dramatic story.

Stanley arrived in Zanzibar in January 1871, full of youthful optimism, and set about organizing his expedition, equipping it extravagantly. He purchased six tons of supplies, including 29,000 yards of assorted cloth, 350 pounds of copper wire, and a huge assortment of beads to trade with the natives. He also acquired a number of articles hitherto not considered essential to African exploration such as a bear skin, a Persian carpet, a bathtub, silverware, kettles for cooking, and a bottle of rare champagne to drink with Livingstone when they met.

Stanley told no one at Zanzibar that he had come to find Livingstone. The truth, and Stanley was not eager to publicize it, was that he had been sent to get a story - and get it any way he could. Bennett had told Stanley, "If he is dead, bring back every possible proof of his death." Those were Stanley's instructions when he sailed for Africa.

Americans abroad were looked on condescendingly at that time. And since Stanley had rid himself of his Welsh accent, he was assumed to be an American heading an American expedition. Because he seemed American, none of the Europeans in Zanzibar really thought he would survive his journey into the African interior. But this cocky little man with the barrel chest and hypnotic gray eyes was extremely gifted. Within the next six years, he was to take a place beside Mungo Park and Livingstone himself in the annals of African exploration.

Stanley's first expedition followed the old trail of Burton and Speke. Aside from the help he brought Livingstone - which was considerable - this journey was important mainly because it made him world-famous and helped turn an intrepid newspaperman into a thoroughly tested explorer. Because of his initial inexperience, the fact that he got through at all was remarkable. His success was great compared with the even greater possibility of failure.

It took him nine months to reach Ujiji, during which time he frequently displayed a physical and moral courage that was worthy of any of his predecessors. However, as he confessed in his book, *How I Found Livingstone,* when he at last approached the old man on the flank of a hill overlooking Lake Tanganyika, he was terrified. He knew of Livingstone's Scottish reserve and of the old explorer's undoubted contempt for publicity, so he approached with caution and with fear. As he said, he wanted to rush forward and throw his arms about the doctor, but he was afraid of being rebuffed. So he exercised some reserve of his own and because of this made the moment of their meeting immortal.

After he and Livingstone had exchanged greetings, Stanley ordered the bottle of champagne served. As he handed Livingstone a silver goblet, he said, "Doctor Livingstone, to your very good health, sir." Still rather dazed, the old man raised his drink and replied, "And yours."

The two men stayed in Ujiji for a few weeks while Livingstone rested and gained back some of his strength on the food Stanley had brought him. Finally, the old man decided to accompany Stanley to Tabora. He agreed to wait there while Stanley journeyed to the coast, outfitted another expedition, and sent it back so Livingstone could resume his exploration into the interior.

Stanley and Livingstone reached Tabora after a two-month journey, and on March 14, 1872, they said goodbye. Stanley had to force back tears as he turned and marched away. He had spent four months and four days with the doctor. During this time, as he reported in his diary, he had been "indescribably happy." And during this time, as he was to realize later, his fascination for Africa had grown immensely. The mystery of her lakes and rivers had begun to absorb him. He would remain thus absorbed for the rest of his life.

In August 1872, the porters and provisions that Stanley had sent from the coast reached Tabora. Now Livingstone, patiently awaiting them, could lead a new expedition southwest into Northern Rhodesia. Here he hoped to find a feeder stream that would flow toward the Lualaba. And he hoped in earnest that the Lualaba would flow eventually into Lake Albert - because if it did, then the river might well contain the secret of the White Nile's origin. However, he could not help being afraid that the Lualaba might feed into the Congo River, not the Nile. His health was failing. He had every reason to turn back - except that he had his heart set on establishing the true source of the Nile.

By April 29, 1873, Livingstone had grown so weak he had to be carried. It must have been clear to him by now that he would never finish the last task of his life. But when he died the next night - on his knees in prayer, by his bed - he had given Stanley the key to solving the last riddle of Central Africa: the course of the Lualaba-Congo River.

9
STANLEY'S WAY

When Henry Morton Stanley came back from Africa, he was one of the most talked-of men in the Western world. Queen Victoria gave him a jeweled snuffbox, and America gave banquets in his honor; he basked in wild acclaim. There was even a play about him called *King Carrot,* which was presented in New York. But accompanying the cheers was a distinct undertone of derision - just loud enough to mar Stanley's triumph.

It was widely thought that Stanley had gone to Africa merely to make a name for himself. He had not been motivated by any particular desire to fight the slave traders or explore the wilderness. He had been sent to get a story; thus, he was often regarded as an exploiter, not an explorer. And people were saying that if he could be a hero, anyone could be. Some even said that he had not really discovered Livingstone, but that Livingstone had discovered him.

It was the faint sound of laughter, rather than the cheers, that rang in Stanley's ears when he returned to Africa late in 1873. This time, he was assigned to cover Britain's wars against the Ashanti tribes in the west - in present-day Ghana. The following April, on his way back to Europe, Stanley learned that Livingstone was dead and that what remained of his body was being taken to England for burial in Westminster Abbey. Stanley hastened to London to act as one of the pallbearers.

At this point, a thought struck him. If he were to return to Central Africa on his own to finish Livingstone's work, no one would dare to laugh at him again. Peevishly he wrote: "What I have already endured in that accursed Africa amounts to nothing in men's estimation. Surely if I can resolve any of the problems which such travelers as Dr. Livingstone, Captains Burton, Speke, and Grant, and Sir Samuel Baker left unsettled, people must need believe that I discovered Livingstone."

Stanley received financial support from the *New York Herald* and the London *Daily Telegraph,* but this time, he was traveling primarily as an explorer rather than a journalist. And in this venture, he proposed to accomplish twice what anyone before him had done.

First, he would follow Speke and Grant's route to Lake Victoria to ascertain that this big lake was just one body of water and that the stream flowing from it at Ripon Falls was its only outlet. Then he would go south to make a final test of Burton's theory that Lake Tanganyika contained the elusive source of the Nile. After mapping the entire coast of the lake, he planned to strike west to take up Livingstone's uncompleted work on the Lualaba River. He hoped to follow the Lualaba to either the Mediterranean or the South Atlantic, depending on whether this river flowed into the Congo or the Nile.

Stanley was determined to settle the remaining doubts about the sources of the Nile and to record the entire pattern of lakes and rivers in Central Africa. For his staff, he recruited two brothers - Edward and Frank Pocock, "young English boatmen of good character" - and a young clerk named Frederick Barker. In September 1874, he reached Zanzibar and began preparing the expedition. For lake and river travel, he planned to use a forty-foot steel boat, the *Lady Alice,* which had been built in sections so that it could be carried overland when necessary.

Many of the men of Stanley's African staff had accompanied him on his previous expedition. When they learned the route he was now planning to follow, they were understandably anxious. The trip might take as long as ten years, they said. But Stanley assured them it would take far less time than that. And, as it turned out, he was right.

Stanley assembled eight tons of material for the expedition and hired more than 350 men to haul and guard it. They left Zanzibar for the mainland on November 12, 1874. Stanley was better equipped than he had been the first time. However, as he knew, this did not necessarily guarantee success. Within two months, Edward Pocock died, and he was followed a short while later by Frederick Barker. Disease and desertion took an enormous toll of Africans, until at last, only half of the original number was left - along with Frank Pocock and Stanley, who pushed gamely onward.

Arriving at Lake Victoria in March 1875, Stanley set out by boat with some of his men. Within fifty-seven days, the explorer had sailed 1,000 miles all around the lake. He had proved that Lake Victoria was a single body of water with but two rivers flowing into and out of it: The outlet was the Victoria Nile; the inlet was the Kagera River, which entered from the west.

Stanley's discoveries at last confirmed the importance of Speke's explorations. Stanley wrote that he felt compelled to "give [Speke] credit for having understood the geography of the countries we traveled through better than any of those who so persistently opposed his hypothesis."

From Lake Victoria, the expedition moved south to Lake Tanganyika, which Stanley proceeded to explore thoroughly. When he had finished, he was absolutely certain that Livingstone had been right and that there was no important river flowing out of it, nothing that could possibly be suspected as the source of the Nile. Against this evidence, Burton's theories finally collapsed, and Speke's concept of the geography of Central Africa was completely substantiated.

Now Stanley shipped the men of his party across the lake and led them toward the Lualaba River. He was close to unlocking one of nature's final secrets in Africa: He was to follow the mysterious Lualaba and find out at last where it led.

In October 1876, the expedition arrived at the confluence of the Luama River and the giant Lualaba. Heading downstream to Kasongo, some miles above Nyangwe, Stanley met the notorious slave trader Tippu Tib. This man was said to have taken his name from the sound of spraying bullets. He was half African and half Arab, and was then one of the most feared men in all East Africa. Sixteen years later, in fact, he was close to becoming master of the entire Congo but was finally defeated by the forces of Leopold II, king of the Belgians. If Tippu Tib had known that Stanley would one day be responsible for bringing Belgians, as well as other

European colonists, into the Congo, their meeting might not have been so cordial.

Stanley was eager to know what obstacles there were to a journey downstream. He suspected, of course, that the greatest obstacle might be Tippu Tib himself. Although the Arabs had not yet penetrated deeply in the Congo, they considered it their zone of influence, and they were not especially pleased to see a foreigner there. There had been others besides Livingstone who had stopped at Nyangwe, never continuing down the Lualaba. The question in Stanley's mind was why.

Tippu Tib gave the excuse that he had not wanted to see Dr. Livingstone's health endangered. This was something of an understatement because as Stanley was soon to learn, most of the people who lived downriver were cannibals.

But Stanley was determined to go there. The slave trader argued that he lacked the manpower for such a journey, and also that he did not want to take the risk. Stanley silenced these objections by offering $5,000 if Tippu Tib would take him sixty marches in any direction. Tippu Tib, guided by his strong instinct for making money, agreed.

That night, Stanley called Frank Pocock into his hut for pipes and coffee. "Now Frank, my son, sit down," said Stanley. "I am about to have a long and serious chat with you. Life and death - yours as well as mine - hang on the decision I make tonight." The choice was this: Should they go north, daring the Lualaba, and hopefully gain glory, or should they go south to the safety of Katanga and give up this extremely perilous phase of their quest?

They tossed a coin, an Indian rupee: heads for the river, tails for Katanga. Six times in a row, the coin turned up tails. Disappointed and unsatisfied, the men drew straws: long for north, short for south. Each time they drew only short ones. At last, Stanley said, "It's no use, Frank. We'll face our destiny despite the rupees and the straws. With your help, my dear fellow, I will follow the river." So they threw away the straws, and with them, Frank Pocock's last chance of ever getting home to England.

On November 5, 1876, they left Nyangwe and headed north overland to bypass the rapids that blocked them from the lower reaches of the river. Suddenly they found themselves in a thick forest that was sometimes so dark that Stanley could not see to make notes. And when they occasionally came out on a hill, they could see nothing but forest around them. Tippu Tib began to grumble because they were also being harassed by pythons, green vipers, puff adders, and howling baboons.

At last, in December, when they had gone about 200 miles beyond Nyangwe, the slaver announced he was quitting. He had not yet fulfilled his contract but he demanded to be paid, and there was nothing much Stanley could do about it. He knew if he refused, Tippu Tib was in a position to lure most of his men away.

Stanley's trip down the Lualaba, past the seven cataracts that end at the present town of Stanleyville, was an unrelieved horror. For many months, he had no idea where the river might take him. But though fearful and apprehensive, he could not turn back. He had to complete what he had begun.

Stanley and his men set out on the river on December 26, and for the next month, they were plagued by the assaults of native tribesmen who wanted to eat them. The first time the party was attacked, the explorer withheld his fire. But at last, he found it necessary to clear the river of the native canoes that surrounded the *Lady Alice* and the smaller boats the party also used. During the first days of the new year, the men fought no less than five encounters with the cannibals.

One battle lasted for three hours, and though no one in the party lost his life, the prospect of having to endure similarly terrifying encounters in the months ahead was most discouraging. So was the necessity of overcoming the physical obstacles that lay ahead: the seven mighty cataracts.

When the expedition reached the first of these, the boats were hauled two miles overland on a path that the men cut through the forest and scrub. By

January 8, the waters of the river were calm again, and the party returned to its boats. But by evening, the second cataract lay dead ahead, and more hostile natives were gathering in force.

During the next four crucial days, Stanley displayed his deep faith in himself and the amazing stubbornness for which he had already become known. He repelled the natives and drove them from their villages. Then he organized pioneer battalions that worked night and day to cut a three-mile path through dense forest and circumvent the cataract. While the men worked, Stanley's weary rear guard fought off great hordes of attacking cannibals.

By January 20, the men had cut their way around the sixth cataract. They were now almost exactly on the equator, and they felt confident they would have smooth sailing ahead. But four days later, they heard the booming of another stretch of rapids - the seventh cataract - and the whole company was in despair. Now Stanley paused to take an altitude reading. By testing the boiling point of water, he was able to discern that they were 1,511 feet above sea level. This was about fourteen feet below the known level of the Nile at Gondokoro, much farther north. Now there was little doubt. Stanley and his party were on the Congo, not the Nile. This was dispiriting. If they had been on the Nile, some sort of aid could have been expected to reach them in a matter of weeks. On the Congo, they knew they had many more months of travel ahead, and perhaps hundreds of rapids to overcome.

By January 28, Stanley had skirted the last major obstacle, the seventh cataract. Although he did not know it, his way was clear now for 1,000 miles. There would be no more geographical obstacles until the party reached another series of rapids on the lower part of the river, near the present city of Leopoldville. But there were obstacles, nonetheless: more angry tribesmen eager to do battle with the strange and frightening white men.

During a 100-mile stretch, Stanley and his men fought eight pitched battles. Their stock of ammunition was almost depleted, and they were running out of weapons, but actually their most potent weapon was Stanley himself. He held his party together by the sheer force of his personality. And like Livingstone, he was not above threatening to fire on his men if they became frightened enough to scatter and flee.

The men stayed with him, but the continual combat wearied and embittered them. Sometimes they had only a few hours' peace a day. At one point, Stanley wrote in his journal: "Livingstone called floating down the Lualaba a foolhardy feat. So it has proved, indeed, and I pen these lines with half a feeling that they will never be read by any man . . . Day and night we are stunned with the dreadful drumming which announces our arrival and presence on their waters. Either bank is equally powerful. To go from the right bank to the left bank is like jumping from the frying pan into the fire."

Fortunately, the situation did not last long, and soon the tribes they met along the river were less aggressive. One day they asked a friendly native chief what this river was called, and he replied, "*Ikutu ya Kongo.*" Stanley had compiled a glossary of words of the local language, but he did not need to be a linguist to know what the chief was saying. Nor was he very much surprised.

By March, the party was only about six degrees longitude from the known mouth of the Congo River - about 450 air miles - quite close to it considering the great distance the men had already covered. But they were still more than 1,000 feet above sea level. Obviously, there were treacherous falls and rapids ahead of them before they could reach the sea. There would be no more bouts with native tribes; now their bitterest enemy would be the river itself.

At this point, it was important that they devise some means of holding back their boats from the rushing waters. They learned eventually to use rattan hawsers (thick rope) to leash each boat; the men walked along the shore holding tight to the leashes, and the boats were saved from the river's fury. This system worked well on the shorter stretches of rough water, but frequently, the boats had to be pulled out and carried overland.

Despite these precautions, their supplies were dwindling - more by loss than consumption - and they could not help losing a boat now and then. At one particularly violent section of river, a seventy-five-foot canoe was jerked from the fifty pairs of hands that leashed it, and it swept away. And on April 12, the sturdy *Lady Alice,* containing most of the supplies, and Stanley himself, was torn loose from its cables and whirled several miles through the turbulent river. When the ship was finally shunted into calm waters, Stanley was rescued. For hours, his men had feared he was dead. He was a hard-driving disciplinarian, but after serving him for nearly three years, they had developed a genuine fondness for him.

Some days later, the group came to a great rapids that plunged through a deep chasm. It would have been impossible to follow the river at this point, but an overland route seemed impossible. The banks on either side of the river rose so steep to be impassable. But Stanley managed to coerce some nearby tribes to help him and his men, and together they moved the entire caravan over one of the tall embankments at a rate of 500 to 800 yards a day.

In the meantime, Frank Pocock had begun to suffer from ulcers on his feet. At one set of rapids, Stanley left him behind to be carried overland in a hammock. This seemed shameful to Pocock, so after Stanley had gone ahead, he insisted on traveling the dangerous stretch in a boat. The boat capsized, and Frank Pocock drowned. His body was recovered some days later, and Stanley was grief-stricken.

The young man's death was a blow to everyone. With Frank gone, the men simply lost spirit. They felt sure they were going to die anyway, so why should they continue draining their energy in such a futile endeavor? When Stanley's boat broke loose again and was spun downstream in the rapids, the men were certain he was doomed. And by this time, they were so exhausted that they hardly cared. They would follow him to oblivion soon enough, they thought. But suddenly, Stanley was spotted walking back along the shore, looking as cocky as ever; they could not help being heartened. Perhaps they would make it after all if they stayed with him. So onward they went, following their leader.

By the end of July, the boats had to be abandoned, and the men were traveling overland again. Now they were desperate for food, and they had almost nothing of value left to buy it with. And what was worse, they knew they would get very little for their trading goods because here, near the Portuguese settlement on the coast, only rum and modern weapons were considered valuable.

A few days later, they became so weak from hunger they could not go on, though help lay but a few miles ahead. Stanley finally persuaded a chieftain to carry a letter forward to Boma, or Embomma, and wrote this message by the light of a lamp made of rotted sheeting dipped in palm butter:

Village of Nsanda, August 4, 1877

To any Gentleman who speaks English at Embomma

Dear Sir,

I have arrived at this place from Zanzibar with 115 souls . . . We are now in a state of imminent starvation. We can buy nothing from the natives, for they laugh at our kinds of cloth, beads, and wire. . . . I am told there is an Englishman at Embomma, and as you are a Christian and a gentleman, I beg you not to disregard my request . . . [I want] fifteen man-loads of rice or grain to fill their pinched bellies immediately . . . The supplies must arrive within two days, or I may have a fearful time of it among the dying . . .

Yours sincerely,

H. M. Stanley, Commanding Anglo-American Expedition for Exploration of Africa

P.S. You may not know my name; therefore I add, I am the person that discovered Livingstone in 1871. H.M.S.

Help came from Boma a few days after Stanley's letter was sent, and on August 12, 1877, the entire party reached the Atlantic. They had been traveling 999 days - nearly three years. But their journey was not over. Stanley had made a pledge that if he survived the expedition he would return his men to Zanzibar. He acquired a ship and sailed around the Cape of Good Hope into the Indian Ocean. He deposited the survivors of his expedition at Zanzibar, as he had promised, and then proceeded to England.

Stanley was to return to Africa several times more, but this expedition marked the peak of his career as an explorer. For in a single river-journey, he had succeeded in solving what remained of the mystery of Africa's waterways. Now there could be no doubt: The Lualaba, which rose in Northern Rhodesia, joined the Congo and flowed across Africa to the South Atlantic; and the White Nile rose in Lake Victoria, was joined by waters of the Blue Nile, and meandered north through the Sudan and Egypt to the Mediterranean.

The continent's four great rivers - the Zambezi, the Niger, the Nile, and the Congo - had now been explored, their courses traced entirely. There were still blank spaces on the map, but much fewer than before, and no great geographic puzzles remained to be solved. Exploration continued far into the twentieth century - in the mountains and deserts and into the dark, forbidding jungles. But it can be said that when Henry Morton Stanley returned to Zanzibar on November 26, 1877, three years after he had left it, the great age of African discovery was completed.

Made in the USA
Columbia, SC
08 February 2020